She Wondered If She'd Just Imagined That Night In Sydney, Two Months Ago.

Cal Prescott stood in the doorway, broad and immaculately dressed in a dark grey suit, a chilly gleam in his eyes. Those same eyes had creased with serious concentration as they'd shared hot, wet kisses in the privacy of his penthouse suite. Flared with hunger as he'd slipped her dress from her shoulders—

She slammed the door on those memories, barely managing a croak. "Cal."

"Ava." Cal's voice, a slow burning rasp that had turned her on so quickly, so completely, was the same, but little else was. His face was a study in frozen control, eyes reflecting only an impersonal razor-sharp study as he remained still, somehow dwarfing her kitchen even from the relative safety of the doorway.

She was alone with Cal Prescott. Again.

Dear Reader,

Just like my navigation skills, sometimes my stories begin in one place then end up somewhere completely different. This one was no exception. I did know a few things—secret pregnancy, forced marriage, outback business in trouble—but that's where the similarities ended. Cal and Ava started with different names and occupations, different pasts and conflict, and even though I loved that story, it just wasn't the right one for them. And because I never throw my ideas away, the original version is sitting in my filing cabinet, waiting for its time to shine.☺

It's exciting to see my first "outback" story come to fruition. Even though Gum Tree Falls and Jindalee are purely fictional, I did do some research in and around far western NSW where Ava grew up (no hardship—it's gorgeous country). Creative license is a beautiful thing, so I renovated "The Toaster"—the controversial but expensive apartment block at Sydney's Circular Quay—into a very tall, very elegant building where Cal lives. I don't know about you, but I'd love to have the Quay, Opera House and Royal Botanical Gardens as my daily room with a view!

Come and visit me at www.paularoe.com, where there's more behind-the-scenes info about *The Magnate's Baby Promise*.

With love,

Paula

PAULA ROE

THE MAGNATE'S BABY PROMISE

Silhouette

Desire

Published by Silhouette Books
America's Publisher of Contemporary Romance

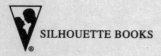

SILHOUETTE BOOKS

ISBN-13: 978-0-373-76962-9

Recycling programs for this product may not exist in your area.

THE MAGNATE'S BABY PROMISE

Books by Paula Roe

Silhouette Desire

Forgotten Marriage #1824
Boardrooms & a Billionaire Heir #1867
The Magnate's Baby Promise #1962

PAULA ROE

Despite wanting to be a vet, choreographer, hairdresser, card shark and an interior designer (though not all at once!), Paula ended up as a personal assistant, office manager, aerobics instructor and software trainer for thirteen years (which also funded her extensive travel through the U.S. and Europe). Today she still retains a deep love of filing systems, stationery and traveling, although the latter is only in her dreams these days.

Paula lives near western Sydney's glorious Blue Mountains with her family, an ancient black cat and a garden full of rainbow lorikeets, magpies and willy wagtails. You can visit her at www.paularoe.com.

Grateful thanks to my wonderful writing group,
The Coven, for the hours of brainstorming,
encouragement and Saturday morning brunches.
Oh, and for letting me immortalize your names in print.
☺ I owe you all a large, decaf soy caramel latte!

One

It's my company. Mine.

The mantra throbbed in Cal Prescott's brain until, with a growl of frustration, he slammed his palms on the desk and shot to his feet.

Victor had really done it this time—not only pitting his sons against each other for the ultimate prize of VP Tech but demanding an heir in the bargain. With a sharp breath Cal whirled to study the panoramic view of Sydney's Circular Quay and Botany Bay below, the gun-metal arch of Sydney Harbour Bridge nestled comfortably in the foreground. The unusually sunny June morning did nothing to smooth his anger; Victor's trademark directness still smouldered away in his gut.

You must both marry and produce an heir. The first one to do so gets the company.

Zac, his stepbrother, didn't deserve VP Tech. He was Victor's real flesh and blood, yes, but the younger man had turned his back on them years ago. It was Cal who'd stuck with family, who had put in the long hours, steadily growing the business until his One-Click office software package had finally cracked the biggest seller spot in Australia last year.

Cal Prescott didn't walk away. Ever. He'd put every waking hour, every drop of sweat into his stepfather's company. Damned if he'd let it slip through his fingers now.

With long-legged strides he stalked over to a discreet wall panel and jabbed a button to reveal a well-stocked bar. He smoothly poured himself a glass of whiskey, neat.

Making money, proving himself, had been an all-consuming desire for so long he barely remembered a time he hadn't lived and breathed it. And with every million he'd made, every deal he'd brokered, he could've sworn he'd seen pride on Victor's craggy face, felt the rush of approval when the gruff, emotionally spare man imparted brief praise. Obviously he was good enough to bring in millions but not good enough to be a Prescott, to be automatically entrusted with the legacy of VP Tech.

Unfamiliar bitterness knotted his insides, curled his lip. Victor hadn't even given him the courtesy of an explanation; he'd simply issued the ultimatum then left on some business trip, leaving Cal to sort through the bombshell's wreckage.

The phone rang then and Cal sat, grabbing the receiver.

"There's a woman I'd like you to meet," Victor said by way of greeting.

Speak of the devil. "You're back."

"Yes. You remember Miles Jasper, the Melbourne heart surgeon?"

The sour taste of futility burnt the back of his throat. "No."

Victor ignored him and continued. "He has a daughter. She's twenty-seven, blond, attractive and—"

"I don't give a damn if she's Miss Universe," Cal ground out. "I'm not some prize stallion at auction. I may have agreed to this ludicrous arrangement, but I *will* pick my own wife." He slammed the phone down with a satisfying crack.

After a long, drawn-out moment he dragged in a controlled breath, slid a sealed envelope from his desk drawer and slowly centred it on the desk with meticulous care.

Thanks to a local investigator and a helpful cabbie, his obsession with the elusive Ava Reilly could now be put to rest.

For the past nine weeks he'd refused to think about *her*, about that one amazing night, shoving it from his mind with the decisive efficiency he was renowned for. But now, as he let his thoughts wander back to their chance encounter, the walls began to crack.

Long limbs, soft black hair and a pair of bright blue

eyes teased his memory. *Ava.* A movie-star name, one that evoked a woman with poise, elegance. Presence.

She'd gotten under his skin and stayed there, disrupting his thoughts at awkward times—in meetings, with clients. The worst were the early mornings, before the sun rose. Time and again he'd hauled himself from the depths of a hot erotic dream where her mouth had been on his, her lips trailing over his chest, her skin hot and silky beneath his hands. It had left him frustrated and aching with need way too many times.

He'd been determined to forget her, forget what had just been a one-night stand. Ironically, he'd gotten his wish three days ago. Three days since his stepfather had issued his ultimatum, seventy-two hours in which VP Tech had dominated his thoughts and he'd seesawed between dull, throbbing rage and aggravated tension.

With a flick of his wrist, he ripped open the envelope and scanned the report.

After too many broken nights and unfocused days, he'd taken action. Now he steeled himself for reality to shatter the fantasy. She could be married, or engaged. His thoughts darkened. He could've been her last fling before she'd settled down to marry her childhood sweetheart—

As his eyes flipped over the paragraphs, his brows took a dive. Ava Reilly owned a bed-and-breakfast in rural western New South Wales.

He reached for his computer mouse, clicked on the Internet connection and typed "Jindalee retreat" in the search engine. Seconds later he was looking at Jindalee's basic Web page. No wonder she was up to her eyeballs in debt with the bank about to foreclose next month. The place was under-promoted and unremarkable for a simple outback town with less than five hundred people.

He went back to the report, skimming over her financials until he got to the summary of her weekly errands. Cal snorted. That PI was thorough, he'd give him that.

Approximately eight weeks pregnant.

"What the hell?"

Office walls suddenly closed in on him, tight and airless, forcing Cal to take a deep gulp.

In one sharp movement, he crushed the offending paper and hurled it across his office, where it hit the wall with a soft thud. *No. No way. Not again.*

A shuddering breath wracked through him as shock stiffened every muscle. He'd had that, once. A baby. *His baby.* A child to follow in his footsteps, to nurture and love. To shower with his wealth and experience and to ensure the past was never repeated. He'd been ecstatic when Melissa had told him. Vulnerable.

Stupid.

She'd faked everything and he'd vowed never to repeat that failure again.

But this...*this* changed everything.

He tightened his jaw, teeth grinding together. After making mad, passionate love, Ava had run like a thief in the night. If not for those black bikini knickers he'd found tangled in the sheets, it could have all been just a delicious, erotic dream.

His thoughts spun out of control, fed by heated memories. And as he recalled every sigh, every touch, his shock morphed into something more sinister. Swiftly his mind clicked through options. Chance encounter or deliberate? Perhaps part of a calculated blackmail plan?

His harsh laugh exploded in the quiet office. If the child *was* his, it provided a neat solution to all his problems.

He slammed down his glass then picked up the phone. "Jenny—arrange for a car and inform the airstrip I'll be flying within the hour."

Replacing the receiver with deliberate slowness he stood, a low curse softly rumbling across his lips.

His baby.

Shards of intense possessiveness stabbed, threatening to choke off his air. If Ava thought he'd pay up and stay out of her life, she was very much mistaken. Every single day, in the midst of everything he'd attained, who he was and where he'd come from were never far from his mind. And no long-legged, dark-haired seductress with wide blue eyes would compromise his beliefs.

With gnawing apprehension, Ava realized she had to face facts—Jindalee was spiralling into a money pit and she had no way of stopping it.

She sighed, eyeing the final notices spread before her on the kitchen table. Absently she ran a frustrated hand over the tangle of hair that had slipped from its ponytail. She'd been certain people would jump at the chance to spend time at a real get-away-from-it-all rural retreat, so certain she'd sunk all her parents' insurance money into the venture. She'd converted the homestead into a reception and dining area, built a five-cabin extension and refurbished the kitchen.

All to emphasise her spectacular downfall.

Her rooms were empty most weekends and she didn't have the money or experience to keep on advertising. Despite her fierce determination to ignore the town gossips, she knew they'd feed on this until her belly started to grow, and then the Gum Tree Falls grapevine would be buzzing anew with "have you heard the latest on Ava Reilly?"

With burning cheeks she stood, eased out the kink in her back and took a deep breath. Tentatively, she placed a hand on her still-flat stomach.

A baby. Hers.

Wonder and shock tripped her breath, adding a shaky edge to the inhale. She tried to swallow but tears welled in her eyes. Quickly, she dashed them away. She hadn't gone looking for a one-night stand, yet the stranger had commanded her eyes the instant he'd settled on the barstool next to hers at Blu Horizon, an exclusive cocktail lounge at Sydney's Shangri-La Hotel. He'd radiated confidence and wealth as if powered by some inner sun, from every thread of his sharply tailored black suit to the closely cropped, almost military haircut. Yet there was something more, something a little vulnerable beneath that chiselled face, all angles and shadow.

It was only after she'd snuck back to her girlfriend's

place at 2:00 a.m. that she'd discovered the real identity of the man who'd rocked her world. Mr. One-Click, heir apparent to the great Victor Prescott's vast technology empire. Cal Prescott's computer software had recently become number one in national sales. Hell, she'd just upgraded her office computer with the latest version.

She snorted at the irony. Cal Prescott was one of the richest men under thirty-five, a man who regularly dated supermodels and socialites. He was a man who avoided emotional entanglements, who revelled in his bachelor lifestyle. If working long hours and staying single was an Olympic event, he'd have a cupboard full of gold medals.

It was a good thing you left. A smart choice. The *right* choice. Still, a tiny doubt niggled. How could she single-handedly bring a baby into her life, a debt-ridden life to which she could add the grim possibility of being homeless, too?

She'd wavered between absolute joy and utter despair a million times this past week. And every time she always returned to one realization: fate. Karma. Destiny. Whatever it was called, the universe was telling her that despite everything, this baby was meant to be.

Ava Rose, life never throws anything your way you're not capable of handling. Her mother's favourite phrase teased her mouth into a too-brief smile before the familiar throb of loss hit. She let it sit there for a second before shoving it aside. Death and tragedy hadn't defeated her before. A new life wouldn't now.

She dropped her hands to the table and gathered up the

papers. The pity party's over. It was time to take action and get her life back on track. Somehow.

"Doing your paperwork, I see."

Ava whirled, her brain tingling at the sound of that oh-so-delicious voice. A millisecond later, her stomach fell to the floor.

Cal Prescott stood in the doorway, broad and immaculately dressed in a dark grey suit, a chilly gleam in his eyes. Those eyes, once so intensely passionate, now so cold and distant that she wondered if she'd just imagined that night in Sydney two months ago. Those same eyes had creased with serious concentration as they'd shared hot, wet kisses in the privacy of his Shangri-La Hotel penthouse suite. Flared with hunger as he'd slipped her dress from her shoulders—

She slammed the door on those memories, barely managing a croak. "Cal."

"Ava." Cal's voice, a slow-burning rasp that had turned her on so quickly, so completely, was the same, but little else was. His face was a study in frozen control, eyes reflecting only an impersonal, razor-sharp study as he remained still, somehow dwarfing her kitchen even from the relative safety of the doorway.

She was alone with Cal Prescott. Again.

The air thickened, heavy with expectation. A warm throb started up between her legs as she swallowed a single desperate groan.

"What…" She croaked then cleared her throat. "What are you doing here?"

His lip curled but he said nothing, a broad, tense statue intent on letting the moment swirl and grow. She steeled herself as his eyes flickered over her in thorough scrutiny, gathering up her dignity with a smoothing of her wayward hair. Yet his eyes followed those fluttery movements until she firmly jammed her hands in her back pockets.

He snorted, a sound so full of contempt that Ava took a cautious step backwards.

"Are you pregnant with my child?"

Ava grabbed the edge of the kitchen counter, reeling from the blow. How could he know? She'd barely had time to get used to it herself. She'd driven into Parkes for an over-the-counter test, then followed up at a free clinic. She'd told no one, not even Aunt Jillian.

She opened her mouth but nothing came out. Like an idiot she just stood there, blinking in shock.

"Who…how..?" She finally managed.

"Do not play the innocent, Ava." His eyes narrowed, his jaw tightening imperceptibly. "Now answer me."

The subtle threat behind his silky words, the fury reflected in every tightened muscle, was all too clear. Ava felt her cheeks flush and just like that, she snapped.

"Do you think I *planned* this? I didn't even know who you were until after I—" she paused.

"Ran away?" He finished, his eyes way too perceptive.

She crossed her arms, refusing to let him see he'd struck a nerve. Yet her mind raced a million miles an hour until something finally clicked. "That's why you're here. You think I want money from you." Bile rose in her throat, acrid and burning. "Get out of my kitchen," she ground out.

"I'm not going anywhere. Is the baby mine?"

For one heartbeat, she seriously considered lying, but just as quickly rejected it. Apart from the fact she was a terrible liar, she *wouldn't*. Not about something this important. So with fear of the unknown fluttering in her belly, she slowly nodded. "Yes, Cal. It's yours."

He paused. "A paternity test will prove it."

"Yes," she said firmly. "It will."

His cold mask cracked, morphing into an expression so raw that she had to take a step back from the intensity.

He strode to her, the distance between them evaporating into an excruciating invasion of her comfort zone. He was Cal Prescott, and he was there, *right there* and amazingly, the urge to touch him, to smell him, thundered through her senses. She wanted to melt right into his very bones until she couldn't tell where she finished and he started.

Anger poured off him, slamming into her, breaking through her thoughts. Then with a soft curse he abruptly whirled, shoving a hand through his hair, leaving short, tufted peaks in its wake. Hair that emphasised his ruthlessly angular face and framed those rich brown eyes to perfection. It was a face so achingly distant, one that screamed control and power in every muscle, every line.

"What do you want?" He demanded now, pinning her with sharp intensity.

Instinctively she placed a hand over her belly,

which only succeeded in drawing his attention. Abruptly she shoved her hands back in her jean pockets. "From you? Nothing."

His gaze narrowed. "Don't lie to me. Not now."

"I'm not lying! I didn't even know I was pregnant until a week ago."

"So that's the way you're going to play it." When he crossed his arms, utterly convinced of her guilt, her frustration ratcheted up.

"I don't care what you think," she hissed back. "It's none of your business!"

He stilled, staring at her, while all around them there was silence, as if the earth itself was awaiting his comeback with bated breath.

Then he smiled. The sheer triumph in that one simple action sent a chilling wave over her skin. It was the smile of a man used to getting his own way, a man who made thousands of million-dollar deals and steamrolled over his detractors. It was a smile that told her he'd won.

Won what?

"You being pregnant with my child is none of my business?" he said now, arching one derisive brow up. "On the contrary. I've given this a lot of thought. That child needs a father. We'll get married."

Deep below the surface, the bombshell exploded, sending shock waves through Ava's insides. Oblivious to the aftermath, Cal flipped open a sleek black mobile phone and dialled. "I've already applied for a wedding licence and my solicitor will finalise the prenup. I dislike large engagement parties so we'll skip that, of course. But I have booked dinner at Tetsuya's with my parents tomorrow night, so—"

Ava finally found her voice. "What are you doing?"

"Hmm?"

"Are you crazy?"

"What?" When he put his hand over the mouthpiece and glared at her like she was some sort of annoying irritation, Ava saw red.

"You can't *force* me to marry you!" She jammed her hands on her hips and shouted the last word, anger surging up to scorch her throat.

Slowly, Cal hung up, forcing restraint into every muscle of his body. Her hands fisted on her hips, hips that curved into the worn denim and came this close to being indecent. His eyes travelled upwards, past the ratty shirt that skimmed her waist, the rolled-up sleeves over tanned forearms, to the low neckline that revealed a smooth expanse of throat.

He finally fixed on her face, a face he'd seen in his dreams, deep in the throes of passion. Her silken black hair was half up, half down, the remnants of a ponytail feathering her jaw. A stubborn jaw that was now rigid with fury.

It was the offer of a lifetime, marrying into the Prescott wealth. He may have preempted her blackmail attempt but she'd still be well compensated. What the hell was she ticked off about? Thrown, he glanced at her mouth.

It did him in, seeing that lush mouth again. Gentle

creases around her lips denoted a lifetime in the sun, but all he could think about was the softness of that flesh when it had teased and tempted him. How she'd placed hot, searing kisses across his chest, trailed her tongue over his belly before—

With a silent curse, he scowled, which only seemed to anger her.

"I am *not* marrying you." She enunciated the words as if he was missing a few brain cells.

He scowled. "Why not?"

Her eyes rounded in incredulity. "Because for one, you don't tell someone you're marrying them, you ask them. Second, we don't even know each other. And third, I don't *want* to marry you."

"I know you need money to save this place. I'm making you an offer." When she remained silent, he turned the screw a little more. "You get your money and I get a wife."

Her breath sucked in. "I don't need your money."

"Because you've got so many other offers, right? Your neighbor...Sawyer?" He lifted his eyebrows mockingly. "He's mortgaged to the hilt." As he watched her face drain of color he said flatly, "What, you didn't know?"

She said nothing, just stared at him with those bright blue eyes full of recrimination.

"The way I see it, you don't have a choice," he said now. "I'll give you until tomorrow to think it through, but we both know your answer."

Ava was speechless, floored by the depth of his arrogance. "If you care so much, then why not just sue for custody?" she finally whispered. "Why marriage?"

"Because I do not ignore my responsibilities." His voice tightened in the spacious kitchen. "Did you intend to tell me about this baby at all?"

She quickly drew a hand over her stomach as the blood rushed from her face. She couldn't think, couldn't even breathe with his ever-watchful eyes, the lingering scent of his warm skin, the aftermath of his luscious voice in the air all around her. "I…didn't think you'd want to know. You're Cal Prescott and—"

"You don't know what I want." Fury flickered, working his jaw. "You walked into my life, spent the night, then walked right out again."

"So this is your way of getting back at me?"

"This is not about you. It's about a child." His eyes dropped to her belly, then up again, his expression unreadable. "My child."

He effectively ended their conversation with a flick of his hand, a white business card between his two fingers. When she didn't take it he slammed it down on the counter. "I'll see you tomorrow."

Almost as if he couldn't stand to remain in her presence a second longer, he turned and stalked out the door.

Two

Ava was still standing in the kitchen, Cal's card clutched in her cold fingers, when her Aunt Jillian walked in with a handful of grocery bags, a warm smile on her weathered face. "Ava, darling, I thought we could have chicken for—"

"Cal Prescott was just here."

Jillian put the bags on the table. "The man you met in Sydney?"

"The same."

Jillian opened the fridge and shoved a block of cheese inside. "Really? Is he interested in staying at Jindalee?"

Ava swallowed. Even though she'd given Jillian the sanitised version, her aunt was a perceptive woman.

"Not exactly. Apparently he thinks I'm trying to black-mail him—and with this place teetering on the verge, I can't say I blame him."

Jillian whirled, her lined face a mask of shock. "Oh, my. That's not good."

Ava sank into a kitchen chair and put her face in her hands. "I don't believe this. And now he…" She sighed. "Jillian, I have to tell you something. Sit down."

Jillian kept right on putting away the groceries. "If it's about you being pregnant, I already guessed."

Lord, did the whole world know? Ava's jaw sagged until she snapped it shut with a click. "How? When?"

"You can't hide a sudden craving for cheese-and-pickle sandwiches. Plus," she gently reached out and smoothed Ava's hair, "your hair went curly. Your grandma and I were exactly the same. It's a Reilly thing." Jillian quickly enveloped her in a hug. "Darling, are you okay with this?"

"Yes." With a relieved sigh, Ava let herself sink into the embrace even as her head spun with the last hour's events. "You're not upset I'm not married?"

"It's not the Middle Ages, darling. And I'm not your father," she added pointedly.

Ava just squeezed Jillian harder. "Cal thinks I did it on purpose," she muffled against the woman's soft shoulder. When Jillian pulled back, Ava avoided her aunt's eyes, unable to face the questions there. "And now he's demanding we get married."

Jillian went back to unpacking. "That's very chival-rous of him, especially in this day and age."

"No, it's not! I can't even begin to list the things wrong with this—we're complete strangers, we live separate lives, have careers, not to mention what the town would say—"

"Oh, my giddy aunt!" Jillian slammed a can of tomatoes down on the counter. "Your business is about to go under, you're pregnant by a rich, attractive, single man—a man who wants to do the right thing and *marry* you—and you're worried about what a bunch of old busybodies would say?"

Ava stared at her, stunned. Her Aunt Jillian was the most easygoing person she'd ever known. She'd never raised her voice in anger, never blown her top.

"You're saying I should marry him?" Ava said slowly.

"I'm saying a child has a right to know his father. From what I've read, Cal Prescott never knew his."

"His mother remarried. He *has* a father."

"But his birth father ran out. 'To know the man, at first know the child.'"

"What?"

"Cal Prescott is a man with obvious trust issues, dear, which can make people do extreme things," Jillian explained as she started unpacking the apples. "I do wish you'd pay attention a bit better." Her face suddenly softened. "Or are those hormones kicking in already?"

Ava sighed. "It is *not* hormones. And don't change the subject." She leaned back in her chair, her mind tossing and turning. "I just don't know what to do."

Jillian rolled her eyes. "You both have something each other wants. So you make a deal."

"Have you not been listening about the whole blackmail thing? The only thing he wants is the baby." She laid a protective hand over her belly. "And he's not getting that."

"Darling, do you think he'd actually try to take away your child?" Jillian asked with a shake of her head. "Sounds to me the man just wants to be a father. And he can save Jindalee into the bargain. Unless…" she hesitated. "You don't want Jindalee."

Ava flushed. Jillian knew her better than anyone, even her own parents. Jindalee land had been in her family for over a hundred years. The sheep station had been her father's dream, a culmination of hard work and town status. Ava had known from a very early age she was a distant fourth in his affections, streets behind the land, her mother, then her younger sister, Grace. The uncompromising man had often accused her of being too wild, too selfish, too carefree. And she'd proved it in spades at twenty when she'd single-handedly destroyed everything.

Not selfish anymore. She closed her eyes, picturing his silvery head held proud, a dark frown set in a face lined with age and the elements. She'd put her own share of worry lines on that face.

Her eyes shot open when Jillian placed a gentle hand on her shoulder. "You don't have to prove anything anymore, Ava," the older woman said softly. "He's gone. He loved this land, but—"

"So do I." It was the simple truth. She loved the gently sloping hills, the craggy gum trees that housed the native corellas and lorikeets. The kangaroos that grazed in the morning mist and the stunning sunsets that spread across the big navy sky. It made her heart expand with joy every day at the sheer beauty of the land. Her land.

"Ava," Jillian said now, her eyes sympathetic. "It doesn't have to be so hard. No one will think less of you if you sell."

"But *I* would." Ava stood, walked over to the counter and began washing the apples. She'd not sunk everything into this property just to see it fail. And if Cal was on the level, then she didn't even have her neighbour's buyout offer as backup.

Hope bloomed, a tiny thread of light bobbing along a sea of uncertainty. She let it sit there for a couple of seconds until caution doused it. Before she charged into any decision, she had to pin down the details. Cal was offering her a chance to save Jindalee. She might be guilty of many things, but looking a gift horse in the mouth was not one of them. It'd be a cakewalk compared to what she'd already been through.

A cakewalk.

On Saturday at 10:00 a.m., after her two paying customers had checked out, Ava knew she couldn't stall any longer. She'd called and offered to drive the twenty minutes to Parkes, but Cal had preempted her. Now as she watched from her porch, a brand-new red Calais slowly made its way down the dirt road. It finally stopped in the small designated parking area, directly below the huge gum tree.

Ava took a breath, then another, dragging in the comforting kitchen smells to give her strength—vanilla, coffee and fresh-baked apple pie, aromas that said "welcome, come on in!"—or so she'd read in a decorating magazine.

When Cal finally unfolded himself from the car, she did a double take. She'd expected expensive casual: a polo shirt, sharply pressed pants, imported Italian shoes. But he surprised her in a pair of faded Levi's, work boots, a brown leather jacket and white cotton T-shirt, the latter hugging like cling wrap, outlining every muscular dip and curve of his chest. Natural command and raw sexuality oozed from his every bone and Ava couldn't help but stare.

He stalked purposefully up her steps with a long-legged stride that indicated he'd no place else to be, his dark eyes shuttered and focused squarely on her. She threaded her fingers once then released them and suddenly the air was filled with his warm, spicy scent.

"Ava," he said, making her name sound sexier than the promise of a hot, wet kiss. Lord, he undid her. Did he remember how in the dark of night, she'd confessed her name on his lips made her want to melt in a puddle at his feet? How he'd sensuously turned that confession against her and sent her body into a whimpering frenzy with every word, every whisper?

She quickly turned and walked in the kitchen door, but not before she caught his mouth twitch for one brief second. She groaned inwardly. He remembered.

Thankful that the warm kitchen disguised her flushed cheeks, she said over her shoulder, "We'll go into the lounge room."

As she led him down the hall, the tide of impending doom tugged at her legs. Her lounge room was welcoming and expansive, with cream walls and pine colonial-style furniture, but she couldn't help but think Cal could buy a place like this a thousand times over. He was decisive, powerful and obscenely rich. If Jillian thought to sell her on all those attributes, she was sorely mistaken. It only proved to her that Cal was unfamiliar with the word "no."

His closed expression pitched her stomach into queasy unrest. This man, with his brooding thoughtfulness and silent staring, who'd stormed back into her life and accused her of blackmail, was a complete stranger to her.

What on earth was she thinking?

She sat on the chaise longue and folded her legs under her, watching as he remained standing.

"I apologize," he began stiffly, "for yesterday. I believe I could have come off a little…"

"Pushy?" she offered, surprised.

"Determined," he amended firmly. "I'm not used to making deals based on…" He ran his eyes over her and for one second, something flared in the dark depths before he shut it down. "…personal matters."

Ava could only stare. When he unflinchingly met her eyes, something clicked. He was actually *embarrassed* at admitting that—a man worth billions, a business genius who was a dead ringer for Russell Crowe and attracted women by the boatload. Yet his expression said he'd rather eat glass than reveal any emotional vulnerability.

Despite herself, despite his demands, she felt a tiny thread of sympathy unfurl. Yet before she could say anything, he crossed his arms and swiftly changed the subject.

"What I'm offering is a business proposition. You need money. In return, the baby—and you—will have the Prescott name and all that entails."

The smooth conciseness of his proposal took her aback for one heartbeat. In the next, she realized exactly what was happening: Sheer brute force hadn't worked, so he was playing his next hand. Calm reasoning. She wondered what he'd try next if she refused. Seduction, perhaps? To her annoyance, a gentle anticipatory buzz tripped over her skin.

"Won't a wife put a downer on your lifestyle?" she said now, shoving those distracting thoughts aside.

His eyes bored into her. "Let me make this clear—you are having my baby. Which means I want *you*."

Hot excitement fired through her veins, steamrolling every other thought into oblivion. She tried to will it away but it kept on coming, a constant pounding wave that alternately thrilled yet alarmed her.

With a deep breath she finally managed to gain some

modicum of control. Cal was simply claiming his child, that was all. He just wanted what she could give him.

So why was she acting like a jittery fool in love?

She dragged her eyes away, her mind spinning. Why couldn't he be the man who'd stormed in her door and accused her of blackmail? At least that way she could refuse his demands with a clear conscience.

Bottom line—losing Jindalee was not an option. And her other choices included bankruptcy and poverty. She also had Jillian to think about; she'd convinced her aunt to sell her little café and come live with her. And Cal was offering more than financial security, a chance to keep the land and ensure the Reilly legacy stayed in the family. He was willing—no, demanding—to be a presence in her child's life. A man who wanted all the responsibilities that being a father entailed.

That was more than a lot of children got these days, herself included.

She finally glanced up, only to catch Cal studying her with an intensity that made her itch to smooth her hair and check her teeth.

"What kind of arrangement did you have in mind?" she said now.

"A legally binding contract. You marry me and in return I'll pay off all your debts, plus give you any assistance necessary to see this place turn a profit."

"I'm not handing this place over to some manager. The land and property remain in my name."

"Naturally. But I do expect you to be in Sydney

whenever I need you, to be available for functions, dinners and such."

"No." Ava swallowed. A quickie wedding was one thing. But to publicly flaunt it, to *pretend*?

He crossed his arms with a small sigh, a sure indication he'd lost patience. "Yes. Did you think I'd just give you money and that'd be it until the child was born?"

"I thought…"

"Well, you thought wrong." His jaw tightened. "This is my stipulation."

Any hope of taking the money and keeping a low profile quietly disintegrated. "So I'm to be your arm decoration."

"My fiancée," he corrected. "You will be my wife, the mother of my child, and I expect you to conduct yourself accordingly. As I will."

She blinked. "Which means?"

"No unscripted interviews, no tell-all book deals if and when we divorce." His eyes suddenly darkened. "And no lovers while we're married."

A surprised breath tore at her throat. "I need to think." Quickly she rose and the room tilted beneath her feet. Just as she grabbed the longue, Cal's hand shot out to steady her.

The shock was so instantaneous, so unexpected, that she gasped. As his long fingers curled around her upper arm, her treacherous flesh caved. A sudden flicker of heat sparked in her belly, sending desire across her skin, making her muscles ache with want.

As if her mind could sense the thin thread of control she teetered on, that night came flooding back in hot, bright technicolor. His eager mouth on hers, on her neck. His sure, skilful hands cupping her breasts, teasing her nipples into peaking hardness. And his hot passionate breath trailing a path of seduction from her navel down to—

She pulled away, refusing to meet his eyes, barely managing a "thank you." Inside, she tried to squelch the spurt of panic but reality crashed in. If she wanted to save Jindalee, she had no other choice.

She rubbed her cheek, surprised at the heat beneath her hand. There was no denying her body's reaction to his simple touch. She wanted him. Even after just one night, after his accusations and demands, she wanted him.

With an inward groan, she crossed her arms. "Fine. After you leave for Sydney I'll keep you updated on the baby's progress. Of course I will—"

"No. I'm flying home this afternoon. You're coming with me."

"Today? That wasn't part of the deal."

Cal paused, as if chewing back his words with infinite patience. "Being my wife means social functions, outings, the whole shebang. Starting immediately. I've also booked you in to see a top paediatrician on Tuesday."

She frowned. "Do I have any say in this?"

"On this, no. Which reminds me…" he flipped open his phone and dialled, exchanged a few words, then hung up. "We'll be back here next Sunday with my team," he said. "They'll need a tour, plus your existing marketing and advertising strategy. I assume you do have one?"

She straightened her shoulders with an indignant glare. "Yes."

"I've also authorised payment of your loans and any other outstanding debts." He shoved his hands on his hips. "Anything else?"

Howsabout you build a time machine and go back about nine weeks? The words bubbled up in her throat but she quickly swallowed them. Mutely she shook her head.

"Ava? Are we in agreement?"

She nearly whimpered as Cal's deep voice flowed over her, kicking up her pulse another notch. *Stop. Please stop talking, before I completely lose it.* Her feet rocked, her heart hammering in her chest.

"What happens after the baby's born?" she said hoarsely. "What if we…decide it's not working?" *What if you decide playing daddy isn't fun anymore? What if I end up hating you? What if you fall in love with someone?* Her heart twisted for a second, surprising her.

"Thinking about divorce before we're even married?" He quirked one eyebrow up and she flattened her mouth until her lips hurt.

"Yes."

He gave her a slow, considering look. "If that time comes, I'm open to discussing it. Not before. I've put a clause in the prenup to address that. But regardless of what we decide, I'm still that child's father."

The underlying thread of possessiveness was undeniable. If that didn't drop her stomach, then the "if the time comes" bit did. Of course the time would come. A country girl and a big-city billionaire were no more suited than chalk and cheese. No one these days based a marriage purely on financial gain. No one except her, that is.

She nodded, even as perverse disappointment rioted through her. "So you're asking me to marry you?"

Cal dragged his eyes away from the hollow of her neck to focus on her eyes. "Does this mean you're saying yes?"

"Are you asking me to marry you?" she repeated, crossing her arms across her chest. Unfortunately, it only drew his attention to her breasts, which were now pushing seductively up from the deep V of her buttoned shirt.

Cal's words inexplicably stuck to the roof of his dry mouth. Then he suddenly recalled their earlier conversation. *He hadn't asked her.* He cleared his throat. "Ava. Will you marry me?"

She took a breath, almost as if drawing in strength. "Yes. But with stipulations."

"Go on."

She flushed but kept right on going. "Any major decisions, any changes concerning Jindalee must be first approved by me."

Cal frowned. "My team is better equipped to decide—"

"This is my land, Cal." She levelled an unwavering gaze at him. "I get the final say-so."

"Okay," he conceded, finally seating himself on the

arm of a sturdy one seater. "I'll have my solicitor put it in the contract."

Ava stilled, waiting for a sign, anything that would let her know she was either making a colossal mistake or doing the right thing. Nothing. And as the seconds ticked by, she took another breath, then sat.

"I plan to be a hands-on mother, which means I won't be handing this baby over to a nanny just so I can swan off to parties with you."

His brief flash of surprise quickly disappeared with a cool nod. "Understood."

"And..." She faltered. "One more thing. The sleeping arrangements." One eyebrow kinked up but he said nothing. Under his scrutiny she felt the traitorous heat bloom across her skin. "I don't think it would be a good idea to...well..."

"Have sex?" He leaned back, carefully crossing his ankle over one knee as his mouth twitched. His nonchalant amusement only deepened her embarrassment.

"Well, yes."

He shrugged. "If that's what you want."

Ava nodded, mortification clogging her throat. Of course it's what she wanted. He thought she was a woman who got herself pregnant just to blackmail him. She had more self-respect than to jump into bed with a man who believed she was a common criminal.

Yet his quick acquiescence seared the edges of her womanly pride. As she studied him, she recalled an article she'd once read...something about pregnant women being a huge turn-off for some men. She'd never pegged Cal for one of those men. But then, they'd been lovers for only one fleeting night—what did she really know about her husband-to-be?

She felt the blood drain from her face. Her husband. To be.

"Then it's settled." He leaned forward, hand outstretched and for a second she just stared at him. At his questioning look, she quickly took his hand, sealing the deal and her fate with one firm handshake.

Yet her mind wasn't on the deal they'd just struck— it was on the way his long fingers wrapped around hers, enveloping her in heat and…something more, something almost protective. Something that tugged at the deepest part of her, that spoke to every teenage yearning, every wish list of happy-ever-afters she'd ever made. Here was a man in every sense of the word—strong, determined, a provider. The sheer command of his very presence took her breath away.

"Ava?"

With a jolt she realized she still held his hand and worse, she'd been stroking it with her thumb.

With a gasp she tried to pull back, but he refused to let her go. Instead she stood but he followed her, his hand still imprisoning hers.

"Ava…" he trailed off, almost as if rethinking his next words.

"Cal, please." Please don't? Or please do? Her head said one thing, her body another, and from the sudden awareness sparking in his dark eyes, she knew which one he'd chosen to hear.

Please do.

He drew her to him with all the skill and confidence of a man who knew she wouldn't refuse. He cupped her elbows, pinning her to his chest, to that warm, hard wall of muscle beneath soft cotton that cried out to be touched, caressed. Kissed.

She closed her eyes as heat and desire turned her brain to mush, waiting in willing anticipation for his lips to claim hers. A tremble started up in her belly, looping and swirling as she felt his warm breath gently swoop over her mouth. Her heart kicked up the tempo, beating hard in her throat, in her head. In a sharp rush, she exhaled, then…then…

Nothing.

"Look at me."

His sinful voice sent a flutter of goosebumps over her skin. Slowly, she did as he asked.

Danger. She felt it crackle in the air as his chest pressed intimately into her breasts. His eyes held the re-membrance of mutual pleasures, everything she'd walked away from, everything in her tortured dreams.

A deep, burning need seared Cal a thousand times over as he stared into her upturned face. To his stunned amazement, he realized he wanted her, right here, right now. After weeks of denial, his body ached for her like he'd been cloistered in a monastery for years. He shouldn't want her. Damn, he didn't even *trust* her.

Pride nipped at his heels, giving him the strength to release her. With regret dogging his retreat, he gritted his teeth.

"If you want me, Ava," he growled, unable to disguise the lust in his voice, "then you'll have to say it."

Three

Her eyes, heavy with arousal, suddenly flew wide open. "What?"

She looked so different from the first time they'd met—more earthy, more sensual. Yet he could still see a glimpse of the woman he'd bedded underneath the denim veneer: the way her eyes tilted up at the corners, the ripe lush mouth that was heaven to taste. Lord, he just wanted to peel off that snug shirt, yank down her jeans and take her with that sexy midnight hair falling around her shoulders, her lips whispering his name.

With a soft curse, he shoved a hand through his hair and gave her his back.

"You want me to ask you for sex?"

The disgust in her voice had him whirling back to the angry indignation tightening her face.

"You actually want me to beg?" She breathed, incredulous. "Of all the conceited, arrogant…! Yes, I've agreed to marry you but I am *not* going to pander to your ego by—"

"Hang on." He put up a hand in alarm. "I never said—"

"—begging you for anything! First you accuse me of blackmail and now this. I get it—it's some sort of punishment for—"

"Stop!"

His command only angered her more. She pulled herself up to her full five-foot-three and jammed her hands on her hips, her face tight with passionate fury. "I will not stop! And just because I'm having your baby doesn't mean—"

"Would you stop yelling at me?" Cal grabbed her arms, shocking them both into silence.

"Let's get something straight," he managed to grind out. "We both know we're attracted to each other—as evidenced nine weeks ago." He thought he detected a glimmer of something in her blue eyes but couldn't be certain. "But I'm not about to force myself on you because some piece of paper says I'm your husband. If you want me in your bed, then it's your decision and yours only. Understood?"

"And what," she whispered hoarsely, her eyes wide,

"makes you think I'd want you when you so clearly don't trust me?"

They remained still for a second, then two. Then, as if she realized he still held her, her arms tensed beneath his hands.

He swiftly backed off, abruptly changing the subject. "We have a flight to Sydney in a couple of hours. You need to pack."

"I have a business to run."

"You also have a family to meet. Don't you have an aunt who can look after this place for a few days?"

"How—" Ava stopped. Cal finding out about the baby was one violation she'd get over. But digging into her past without even giving her the option of what she wanted to reveal? Her mouth felt bitter and dry. Dear lord, what had she gotten herself into?

As if she was standing outside someone else's life looking in, Ava sat on the balcony of Cal's Circular Quay penthouse suite, taking in Sydney Harbour spread out like a picture-perfect postcard thirty floors below.

His place was something out of *Architectural Digest*. The elevator doors had swooshed open to reveal a massive living room in varying shades of cream and white, a warm chocolate couch opposite a solid rustic coffee table in the centre. Along the right wall, separating the bedrooms, ran a stunning tropical aquarium. In silent awe she'd barely registered Cal's brief tour, until they'd walked through the dining area and into an im-maculate kitchen. Too immaculate.

"Do you cook?" she'd asked him. He'd just shrugged and said, "I eat out, mostly."

There was something here for all the senses, she realized. Even on the balcony, the decadent cream cashmere couch felt like heaven against her bare calves, just like the expensive cotton sheets on her guest room bed. The briny ocean breeze left a salty tang on her lips, tainted warmly by the patio heater glowing in the far corner. And through the double glass patio doors floated the soft strains of James Taylor on the CD player, mingling with the faint bustle of Circular Quay below. All that marred the perfection was the absence of an active kitchen. Something simmering on the stove…a lamb roast, she mused, some garlic potatoes, fresh carrots and green beans. Or a Greek salad. Her stomach rumbled in agreement and a small grin tugged at her lips.

Her good humour faltered as Cal appeared at the door with two wine glasses. He'd changed into a dark navy suit, light-blue shirt and a precisely knotted sapphire silk tie, while she had to be content with the cherry-red dress he'd first seen her in. It was a little snug across the breasts but the best she could do on short notice.

"Magnificent, isn't it?" His quiet confidence made it sound like he'd painted the harbour view himself, and she couldn't help but smile.

"Yes."

He studied her, almost as if assessing her against some unspoken criteria. She must have finally passed muster when, with a glint of remembrance in his eyes, he said, "Nice dress."

"My *only* dress," she replied and recrossed her legs. The floaty chiffon hem slid over her skin, baring a long expanse of thigh. Surreptitiously, she rearranged the fabric, but when his shrewd gaze followed her hands, the warmth began to rise again.

To fill the uncomfortable void, she took a grateful swallow of the bubbly lemon, lime and bitters, then grabbed up the paper he'd shoved across the glass table.

It was a briefing paper, not only outlining his business deals but some personal details, details she'd be expected to know as his fiancée. She scanned down the page, unable to stop that rush of morbid curiosity. She knew nothing of him—at least, not the things that really mattered. Deep, personal things she always thought you should know about your husband-to-be. Little intimacies that indicated you were a couple, in love and happy to spend the rest of your lives together.

"You'll be thirty-four on New Year's Day." At his nod, she asked half to herself, "What do you get a man who can afford to buy anything?"

"Something simple. My mother bought me the fish tank last year." At her raised eyebrow, he added, deadpan, "But I can always use a tie or a nice bottle of Scotch."

"A pair of socks?"

She returned his grin with one of her own and for the

first time since arriving in Sydney, Ava felt his full and complete attention. The gentle tug of desire unfurled inside, but with ruthless efficiency, she shoved it back.

On his private jet he'd been engrossed in paperwork and phone calls. The journey to his apartment hadn't been much better. She should have enjoyed the decadent opulence of driving in his shiny black hybrid Maserati Coupé, blanketed in the luxurious smell of leather seats, the throaty purr of the powerful engine as they smoothly glided along Anzac Parade. Yet she couldn't shake the awful thought that this was a premonition of things to come—she silent and immaculately groomed and he the workaholic with always one ear to the phone, one eye on a business deal.

She didn't want to be the wife who paraded about in designer dresses and jewels, a perky, dolled-up hostess serving only to entertain her husband's business colleagues. She shuddered at the thought of putting on makeup day after day, having her hair teased and primped, dressing up like Corporate Wife Barbie.

And stupid, stupid her—she was going to sign a contract that gave him carte blanche.

You have to remember this is just temporary. She'd be at Jindalee most days, focusing on her business. She'd be with Cal only when he needed to show her off and make a good impression. He'd said so himself.

His own personal show pony.

With self-anger dogging her thoughts, she glanced away, back to the darkening sky.

Instead of taking a seat next to her, he sat on the couch directly across the coffee table, thankfully on the outer edges of her personal space. Yet anything short of another city was still way too close. He was simply too commanding to ignore, let alone be comfortable with. It was a combination of the dark, knowing look in his eyes, the sensual flow of his voice and the annoying memories that surged up to goosebump her skin.

She quickly returned her attention to the paper. "You started working for Victor at seventeen and now you're a managing director. Did you…" she paused, mentally rephrasing the question. "You never felt the urge to start your own business?"

"VP Tech *is* my business."

She remained silent at his cryptic statement until he elaborated with a small shrug. "I dropped out of school to work in Victor's software development division. A few years later I had the idea for One-Click and Victor supplied technical staff and financial backing. Today we're the only Australian company with integrated Internet, phone and software technology in the one office program. It brings in billions."

After a brief second she changed gears. "What's your mother like?"

His reply was instantaneous. "Loyal. Generous. Supportive."

"And your stepfather?"

Cal paused, allowing himself the opportunity to study her features, the uptilted nose, the elegant sweep of her cheek. The way she looked genuinely interested in his answer. "Commanding. Immovable. Astute."

"And he won't figure out our newly engaged bliss is a front? Or are you planning to tell them the truth?" she said, her voice in complete control. Yet her eyes gave her away, deep pools of turmoil. Abruptly she glanced down, breaking contact.

"Are you worried about what people will think?" he asked slowly. The small crease between her eyes indicated he'd hit the truth.

"About what your parents will think, yes."

Despite that ever-present distrust that lingered like an early morning fog, the air suddenly shifted, stirred by a gentle wave of something Cal didn't want to explore, let alone acknowledge. Not even to himself.

He barely heard the catch in her breath, but he couldn't miss the struggle etched in the gentle curves of her face. Shoving down that sliver of unfamiliar guilt, he instead focused on his purpose. He'd had one moment of weakness, and it was his responsibility to make it right. He'd learnt that from Victor. He didn't welcome this deep, burning need to have her skin on his, to have her body hot and writhing beneath him.

Yet for the first time in months, he simply wanted.

He ground his teeth together. *Christ.* Now he was hard.

With a determined slant to his jaw, he refocused. Things with Ava were business. They had to be.

The silence stretched until the need to fill it with something, anything, became unbearable. Cal finally broke it.

"If they ask, you can just say we met over cocktails at the Shangri-La, kept in touch and met up again recently."

"But isn't a sudden engagement out of character for you?" she pressed.

"Trust me, they won't ask. At least, my mother won't."

"And Victor?"

He paused, twirling the glass in his hand. "It's none of his business whom I chose to marry. Let me handle him." As his firm command lingered, their gazes clashed, one curious and bright, the other shadowed and dark.

Ava severed it and reached for her glass. "So we're going to fake it."

The unintentional double entendre curved his mouth. "That a problem?"

She looked discomforted by his scrutiny. "I'm not good at deception."

Interesting. "Oh, I'm sure you'll manage. Just think of the money."

He could've kicked himself when an injured shadow passed over her face. But then she turned back to the view and it vanished.

What was with him? He preferred women who understood the demands of his lifestyle, women who were polished, sophisticated, who weren't looking for promises or commitment. Women who could elegantly fake a parental inspection with ease. They'd graced magazines, television, catwalks. They met his needs sexually, socially and mentally, although not one woman had met them all.

But Ava…what was it about her and just *her* that compelled him?

Sure, she was a hot package. Their one encounter still haunted his memory. His eyes dipped to her neckline, to the silky material stretched taut across her breasts. Ava Reilly was also stubborn and proud, qualities that alternately fascinated and frustrated him.

Don't forget she bargained her baby to save her business.

That should be enough to extinguish his craving, but inexplicably, it still simmered. And below that, an unfamiliar urge to know more about her, to unravel the pieces of what his brief report had missed, surged up.

"How long have you been at Jindalee?"

His sudden question snapped her gaze back to him.

"Pretty much my whole life." At his frown she added, "Don't you have all this in a report?"

"No."

She held his gaze, as if trying to work out if he was telling the truth or not. Finally she gave a small sigh. "Jindalee used to be a sheep station, built by my father in the late forties."

"How old are you?"

"I'll be thirty in December. My parents tried for ages to have kids, then they had two girls barely a year apart." She clicked her mouth shut and looked away, indicating that line of questioning was closed.

He frowned. When they married, he'd get sole control of VP Tech, everything he'd ever wanted. He should be focusing on that and only that, not sharing intimate details of their lives. She was just a convenient means to that end. He'd done the right thing, the *only* thing by claiming his child. He didn't need to know the intricacies of her past—just like she didn't need to know about Victor's ultimatum.

"So when is the happy day?" Ava said.

For a second, Cal remained wrapped up in his thoughts, in the remnants of anger still clinging to him like ethereal cobwebs. That anger was a constant confirmation never to fully trust anyone, never to let his guard down. But when he snapped his eyes to Ava's, he felt those spidery webs slowly evaporate.

Quickly he gained control. "As soon as possible. How long does it take to organize a wedding?"

She shrugged. "I don't know."

"Isn't it something women always obsess about?"

She gave him a look. "Sorry, I missed the memo."

She took a slow sip of her drink and his attention zeroed in on those cherry-painted lips as they met the rim of the glass, the small ripple under her smooth skin as she swallowed.

"Money's no object," Cal added with more calm than he felt. "If you want a particular place, a certain church—"

"It doesn't matter."

He studied her with interest. "If you could get married anywhere, where would you choose?"

"I haven't given it much thought."

"Okay." He placed his glass on the table with firm decisiveness. "St Mary's Cathedral for the ceremony," he said, naming Sydney's most prominent historical church. "Then my private cruiser on Sydney Harbour for the reception. How does August the first suit you?"

"That's less than…" she calculated in the pause, "two months away. Why the rush?"

"You have a problem with that?" He eyed her stomach, then nodded. "You'll be five months pregnant, obviously showing…"

"That's not the point," she said tightly. "Aren't there waiting lists?"

"Probably." He quirked up an eyebrow. "I can organize a wedding planner."

That threw her. "No! Okay, August the first it is," she finished lamely. "So, getting back to tonight. Tell me more about your parents."

He let her change direction without comment. "My mother, Isabelle, lived in the Hunter Valley. She met Victor when I was eleven and they married a year later."

"You have a brother," she said.

"Stepbrother. Zac." With all traces of amusement gone, he felt the sudden need for distance. He rose, went to the railing, then turned to face her, his back against the cold metal. "He's three years younger than me and Victor's real son."

She smiled tentatively. "I'm sure your stepfather thinks you're just as—"

"Don't."

Her smile slowly faded. "I'm just trying to—"

"You don't read the tabloids, do you?"

Mutely she shook her head.

"Zac left VP Tech a few years back," he said less harshly. "From what I hear he started up his own company on the Gold Coast."

I stayed. I remained loyal. And yet Victor still insists on playing this stupid game with the future of the company.

"Have you spoken to him?"

"What?" He shook his head, trying to dislodge the remnants of bitterness.

"Have you spoken to Zac since he left?" She studied him way too closely, a thread of concern in her bright blue eyes. "You're brothers. Don't you—"

"No. We need to get going if we're to make our reservation," he said gruffly, glancing away with an odd sense of guilt.

Ava hesitated for a brief second as he held out his hand. When she finally took it and he gently pulled her to her feet, she sucked in a breath. There it was again—the jolt of heat, the quickening of her heartbeat, the low ache of desire in her belly. When she instinctively placed a hand on her stomach, his eyes followed.

"Can you…feel anything?"

The sudden flash of wonder in his face was a low, primeval blow, leaving her breathless. What she felt had nothing yet everything to do with the life growing inside her. Her body was changing, growing, and hot, dark need throbbed through her veins. Her skin itched to be touched, to be kissed. By this man.

And there was no way she'd admit that, not when it'd taken all the control she possessed to recover from that near kiss.

"Just a few...flutters," she managed. "It's normal in the first trimester."

"Do you need anything?"

You. "No."

Ava swallowed thickly as he placed a hand on her back, guiding her into the apartment. *Great. Just great.* How on earth was she going to survive another thirty-one weeks of this?

"Do you have a special diet?"

She closed her eyes briefly as the warm brand of his palm seared through her thin dress. "No caffeine or shellfish. Lots of greens, water. And sleep. I've been spending a lot of time in bed..."

She glanced up, caught his flash of amusement and felt her skin prickle hotly.

Get a grip, Ava! It was just...biological. Hormonal. He was a great-looking guy and her body instinctively responded to that. That's all.

When she reached to grab her wrap draped across the back of his leather couch, she noticed a small velvet box perched on top. Her eyes flew to his.

"To add reality to our newly engaged bliss," he explained, plucking the box from her fingers and flicking it open.

Despite herself, she gasped. There, nestled on a bed of black velvet, was the most gorgeous ring she'd ever seen. It was stunning in its simplicity: a claw-set single teardrop diamond, the gold band studded with tiny emeralds. It must be worth thousands…or more. She hesitated, almost afraid to touch it, until Cal eased the ring from its nest and held it out.

"It's beautiful," she sighed.

"I know." She glanced up, only to lose herself in the dark drug of his unfathomable eyes. Quickly she refocused on the ring, willing her hand not to shake as he slid it over her knuckle. It sat there, winking at her, teasing with its carat-laden sparkle.

"A little loose," he murmured, still holding her fingertips as he ran his thumb over the band. Shivers tripped down her skin and she gently eased away.

"Not for long." At his questioning look, she added, "Weight gain."

"Ahh."

When his mouth tilted, the overwhelming need to kiss him stunned her. It shouldn't be. But there it was.

Her whole body tingled with awareness, making her skin burn from the inside. She'd read about pregnancy hormones heightening a woman's sexual appetite, had laughingly listened to the explicit stories her married girlfriends had revealed. But were those hormones supposed to be *this* intense? Like she had a sudden need to rip off her clothes and demand he ravish her on the floor?

She wanted him. Craved him, even. Like she was a chocolate addict, and one taste just hadn't been enough.

A groan rattled in her throat. She couldn't give in to a moment of weakness, no matter how amazing it promised to be. Sleeping with a man who thought her capable of blackmail would leave a deep and lasting scar, and she'd had enough of those to last a lifetime.

With supreme control she took one step back, away from the warm intimacy that had enveloped them as they stood almost touching. She drew her wrap around her, wishing it were solid armour.

"Shall we go?"

A shutter fell over his face, his nod cool and curt. And just like that, the moment was broken. But dàmn, a part of her wished it hadn't, wished she possessed the world-liness, the detachment to make the first move and bring relief to her growing need.

But as Cal coolly guided her out the door, she'd have to instead focus on the night ahead, and put all her energies into getting through it.

Four

Determined to follow Cal's lead and ignore the whispered glances that accompanied their journey through Tetsuya's, Ava lifted her chin and kept walking, fully aware of his warm, possessive hand on the small of her back guiding her forward. Then they were inside the private dining room and the door was closed with a discreet click.

She got a glimpse of the interior—sparsely elegant, with delicious aromas coming from the warming station at the far end—before Cal looped an arm around her waist. It was an intimate brand of ownership, one that did nothing to quash the butterflies in her stomach, and she itched to squirm away. But then he was saying,

"Ava. I'd like you to meet my mother, Isabelle," and her fate was sealed.

A deep breath calmed her panic, leaving behind nervous anticipation. Isabelle Prescott had to be in her fifties at least, but moved with the grace and charm of someone decades younger. Outwardly, she looked perfect, from the hem of her elegant black knee-length shift dress to the top of her perfectly made-up face, surrounded by a fashionably choppy blond bob. As Ava expected, the woman was manicured, perfumed and dressed like a million bucks. Yet when she tilted up to greet Cal with a kiss, her smile radiated genuine joy.

To Ava's relief, when she turned to Ava that smile never faltered.

"Ava, I'm delighted to meet you. I'm so happy for you both."

She barely had time to be surprised by the older woman leaning in to bestow a kiss to her cheek before Cal introduced Victor and a steely handshake engulfed her hand.

Cal was a man who oozed natural command and confidence, a man used to giving directions and having them obeyed without question. Now she knew where he'd learnt it from. The persona of Victor Prescott was just as large as the real-life man himself. His broad, imposing presence was immaculately suited, his grey hair precisely cut, his moustache trimmed. A pair of intelligent blue eyes summed her up in half a second and, determined not to wither under that gaze, Ava returned his handshake firmly and met it. When he smiled the action didn't quite reach his eyes.

"Congratulations, Ms. Reilly."

What an odd thing to say. She shot a glance at Cal. "For…?"

"For being the woman to finally catch my son. He's been notoriously single for too many years."

A tense look passed between the two men before Cal broke it. He took Ava's arm with firm gentleness. "Let's be seated."

With Cal seated next to her and Isabelle and Victor directly opposite, the meal began. To Ava's surprise, there were no menus, just a discreet waiter serving the first of what was to be ten courses from the restaurant's famous degustation menu.

"Venison, beef." Cal named the tiny helpings on her plate, his murmur soft and intimate in her ear. "The others are fish."

"So, Ava," Isabelle began as she dipped her spoon in the gazpacho. "Are you from Sydney?"

"Born and bred near Dubbo, actually."

"A country girl…I like that." Isabelle smiled. "So a city this size would seem a little crazy to you."

Ava slid a glance to Cal, who seemed intent on her answer. "It's large. Noisy. But," she added quickly with a smile, "very beautiful. Sydney's harbour view is like no other."

As she finished the rest of her bio, Ava was acutely aware of the attention she commanded. The scrutiny that worried her most, though, was Victor's. Reputation aside, the man had a way of intimidating with just a look and the slight raising of an eyebrow. He let Isabelle ask all the questions, only interjecting to question her about Jindalee's past incarnation as a sheep station.

As the meal wore on, and despite the glorious food—**Ava had never** tasted beef so wonderfully spiced before—she sensed an underlying tension settle over their table. She frequently caught a guarded sharpness in Cal's eyes, as if he was waiting for something to happen, for someone to say something. She glanced over at Victor. The man eyed them both with speculation, a look that had frequented the meal. One that had first alarmed but now just plain irritated her.

On the flip side, Isabelle was a genuinely lovely woman. Cal's obvious love and respect shone through like the sun on an overcast day. It was the way her whole face creased with humor when she spoke, the way his expression softened. She was obviously the catalyst between two equally forceful and stubborn males.

"And the poor man was covered in Béarnaise sauce!" Isabelle concluded her anecdote with a laugh, prompting Cal into a deep chuckle. Ava smiled through the tiny pang that speared her, forcing her eyes away. They landed on Victor, only to find him studying her with sharp intensity.

Quickly she dropped her gaze to her plate.

"You don't like seafood?" Victor said suddenly. All eyes went to him, then to Ava's plate, where she'd eaten the salad but left the shellfish.

Ava gave Cal a startled look. "I…"

"No, she doesn't." Cal answered smoothly, placing a warm hand over hers on the table. *Calm down*, the small gesture seemed to say. *I'm here.*

Victor snorted. "Well, I've never known a woman to refuse dessert." His gaze became perceptive. "Chocolate cognac mousse…"

"Ava doesn't drink alcohol," Cal said smoothly.

"…and a superior cappuccino."

"Or caffeine."

Victor slowly raised the napkin to his mouth, dabbed, then folded it precisely on the table.

"I see. So to summarize this evening—you're attractive, single, have no discernible indulgences and run a small business while supporting your aunt and the local community. Do you have any vices, Ms. Reilly, or can I assume you're—" he held her panicky gaze in calculating summary "—absolutely perfect for my son?"

Cal's hand tightened over hers. "Oh, for God's sake, Victor, that's enough. She's—"

"Cal, no," she murmured, urging the well of panic back down.

He glanced at her then continued calmly. "Ava hasn't been well the last few days."

Victor's chair screeched across the floor as he abruptly stood. "Cal—a word?"

Cal nodded, rose fluidly to his feet and followed Victor across the room, out of earshot. Even knowing Cal for just a few days, she could still see something simmer below the well-groomed, polite surface. Something angry and resentful.

Ava's stomach sank, aided by Victor's cynical words, loaded to the brim with innuendo. She stared at her plate as the meal congealed in her stomach. It shouldn't matter what that man thought of her, but it did. Painfully so.

"I hope you're feeling better." Isabelle's hand on her arm startled her and when she met the woman's warm brown eyes, they were fraught with concern.

The little white lie twisted inside. "Just a bug."

"I'm sorry if what Victor said upset you. He's just being protective of Cal. It's nothing personal."

"Well," Ava cleared her throat, emotion clogging it, "it sure felt like it."

Isabelle gave her a small smile. "I know. Victor can be a little…autocratic. Abrasive, even. But he's a man used to running a billion-dollar business. Sometimes it's hard to—" she gave an elegant shrug "—shut that off."

"Can I ask you a personal question?" Ava said impulsively. At Isabelle's nod, she said, "You and Victor are so different…" She paused, not wanting to offend, but the other woman's smile drove her onward. "How did you and Victor meet?"

Isabelle laughed. "We are different, there's no doubt about that. Cal was six when his father ran out. We never married, so there I was, five years later, a single mum and working at a winery on the north coast. Victor was looking to buy it, he saw me serving in the café and—" She trailed off, her face soft with remembrance.

"We fell in love. People scoff at love at first sight, but truly, that's what it was. As you probably know," she added with a sparkle in her eyes. "Like you and Cal, I had no idea who Victor was. He didn't know about my life, about my son. But we fell in love and that was it. We were married a year later, when Cal turned twelve."

Ava couldn't help but smile at the woman's misty-eyed reminiscence. "He swept you off your feet."

"And he didn't take no for an answer—not that I didn't make him jump through a few hoops first." She arched a brow in a woman-to-woman look before taking a sip of her wine.

Ava nodded with a smile and finished the rest of her water. It surprised her that this warm, intelligent woman was married to a man like Victor Prescott. Yet there'd been a few times she'd spotted the cracks in the man's ice-hard facade: When Isabelle had reached out to squeeze his hand and he'd returned the grip firmly. Her animated retelling of a story that relaxed his craggy face, softening the controlled lines. Yet in the next moment, the mask returned and he was back to studying Ava like she was a particularly fascinating bug under his microscope.

Isabelle tapped her hand on the table, bringing Ava's attention to the sparkling wedding set on her ring finger. "Ava, I know it's short notice, but would you like to go shopping with me tomorrow?"

Shopping? She glanced over to where Cal and Victor were still talking in hushed animation, then returned to Isabelle.

"We can buy heaps of shoes, drink cappuccino and people-watch," Isabelle teased, with a gleam in her eye. "Uh!" She gestured with mock severity when Ava opened her mouth. "Don't tell me. You're a handbag girl instead."

Ava laughed then. She wanted to know more about Cal, so what better way to get a handle on him than through his mother? "Sure. Shopping it is."

"Excellent!" Isabelle beamed. "Do you have any preferences?"

"Somewhere…inexpensive?"

Isabelle laughed and laid a hand on Ava's. "Think of it as Cal's treat. He can afford to indulge his fiancée, after all. And I promise we'll find something you love."

"Are you ready to go?" Cal said suddenly. Startled, she glanced up, only to find his expression shuttered down tight. She nodded and rose to her feet.

"No coffee?" Isabelle asked, surprised.

"Can't—early start tomorrow. I'll see you later, Mum." Cal placed a quick kiss on his mother's cheek then nodded curtly at Victor.

"I'll send a car for you at eight," Isabelle said as Cal placed Ava's wrap around her shoulders. "Retail therapy," she added at her son's questioning look. And then Cal was gently but firmly guiding her from the room.

The ride back to Cal's apartment was heavy with expectancy. Ava waited for Cal to reveal what he and Victor had discussed in muted anger at the restaurant, but she was still waiting by the time they'd entered the apartment elevator.

"Are you going to tell me what Victor said?"

As the elevator doors slid closed Cal swung his loaded gaze to her, holding it in silent analysis. Despite the awkward, drawn-out moment, she refused to back down.

He jammed a finger on the top-floor button again. "Victor had doubts about our marriage, our…" his gaze lingered on her mouth, "compatibility. I rebutted them."

Ava felt the sudden urge to lick her lips but instead nibbled on the inside of her cheek. "It looked pretty heated."

He shrugged and went back to staring at the blinking numbers as they ascended. "That's Victor— can't stand people disagreeing with him." He crossed his arms, still focused on the floors. "I suppose you'll need some money."

Ava frowned. "For what?"

"Tomorrow. For shopping."

"If that's your way of offering, then no, thank you."

"I can afford it." He reached into his jacket pocket, pulled out his wallet and flipped it open. "Here."

When she remained still, he impatiently waved the card under her nose.

She blinked then drew in a sharp breath. "Platinum Amex?"

He shoved the card into her hand as the doors slid open.

"Don't get too excited." He indicated she go first. "There's a limit."

"I don't need an allowance," she said tightly. "I'm not some kept woman."

"I didn't say you were."

She slapped the card to his chest as she walked past him, but he snared her arm, forcing her to stop. "Let me make this clear to you, Ava. After tomorrow, the public will know you're my bride-to-be. And the first thing you'll be judged on is your wardrobe."

She frowned and pulled free. "What's happening tomorrow?"

"I'm releasing our engagement announcement to the press. What?" he asked calmly as panic flushed the blood from her face. "The sooner we announce it, the less chance of a leak."

A soft melodic jangle permeated the warm apartment and with a shaking hand, Ava reached into her purse. Pulling out her mobile phone, she turned to the kitchen.

"Hi, Jillian." She tried for nonchalance but after she hung up from her aunt's "just checking to see if you're okay" call, she knew she hadn't fooled either of them.

From the sound of it, Cal was also engaged in a call in the living room. He may have given her privacy but he'd pointedly placed the offending credit card in the center of the breakfast bench. It sat there, glinting in the subtle mood lighting, teasing her with its shiny newness.

She reached out, fingering the bumpy numbers. It wouldn't just be small-town gossip this time—Cal's announcement was sure to make national news. People would be talking, and not just about how she and Cal had met and who "the real Ava Reilly" was. They'd focus on her clothes, her hair, her figure.

She rolled her eyes. Following fashionable trends wasn't an option when she had a business to keep afloat. The clothes and makeup she *did* have were at least three years old. Sunscreen was about as close as she got to moisturiser.

But now…the sudden and inexplicable desire to indulge, to splurge on something impractical and feminine, made her insides ache with longing. Many years ago—a lifetime ago—she'd given in to the frivolous call. When Grace was alive.

"So you've changed your mind?"

As if the card had bitten back, Ava snatched her hand away. Cal stood in the kitchen doorway, his jacket off, sleeves rolled up to reveal tanned, muscular arms. The glow from the track lighting barely brushed him, illuminating the golden hairs on his forearms, glinting across the angular face, throwing him half in shadow, half in light. With a sharp movement, he stuffed his hands in his pockets, patiently awaiting her answer as she stood there like a gawky teenager.

The man was beautiful. Her mind emptied, tongue suddenly dry. As if sensing the small war waging in her head, his mouth tweaked.

"Should I alert the media?" Cal said with deliberate nonchalance.

"What?"

He spread his hands wide, outlining an imaginary

billboard. "'Woman turns down all-expenses-paid shopping spree.'"

Finally, a smile. Despite the brief pleasure that small action gave him, he noticed the sadness that accompanied it.

"Once upon a time I would've jumped at the chance." She shifted from foot to foot before reaching down to pull off her high heels. Two inches shorter, she seemed tiny, more vulnerable somehow. She barely met his chin.

"Grace and I…" she paused, shook her head.

Cal recalled her conversation with his mother. "Your sister."

"I thought you and Victor were deep in a business discussion."

"I have an uncanny ability to multitask."

Her tiny snort of laughter surprised them both and for one moment, the tension lifted.

"Your sister died young," he stated softly.

Her smile dimmed. "She was nineteen." She made to turn away, hesitated and instead fixed him with a steady look. "My mother died three years ago of cancer, my father had a heart attack seven months after that. It's been just me and my aunt ever since." She glanced away so quickly that Cal barely had time to distinguish any emotion in her expression. Vulnerability? Sadness? Her voice reflected neither with her next statement. "Don't you already know everything about me?"

"Not everything." He knew her skin shivered when he kissed that sweet spot on her neck, the way she gasped when he nibbled her earlobe. He knew the way her eyes darkened to a stormy blue when she was all fired up about something, in the throes of passion. But suddenly that wasn't enough.

"I don't make a habit of digging into people's private lives," he said firmly.

The moment lengthened as Cal steadily held her gaze, until he shifted, taking a step closer and the air suddenly flared hot.

"Why did you run?"

He was far from touching distance but Ava's whole body still vibrated with anticipation. She remained motionless, holding her breath. He couldn't know how she'd regretted walking away that night, wondering if things would've turned out differently had she stayed.

She decided on an offhand shrug. "To avoid an awkward morning?"

"Really?"

At his slow, dubious eyebrow raise, irritation flared. "Yes. Despite what you think of me, you were my first and only one-night stand. I thought you'd be relieved not having to deal with the morning after."

"You didn't give me a choice," he said softly.

"Well, welcome to the club."

Ava knew she'd struck a nerve. Surprise flitted across his face before he swiftly smoothed it out. Slowly he crossed his arms, bringing the defined muscles in his shoulders, his biceps, into relief.

Under his gaze bravado seeped out, only to end on a

gasp when her belly fluttered. Her hand flew to her stomach.

"What?" He was by her side in an instant, his hand covering hers in sudden shocking familiarity.

She didn't know what made her more breathless, the tiny life moving inside or Cal's warm palm scorching her belly. When she looked up their eyes locked. And held.

In those seconds, his eyes echoed sheer amazement until he dropped his hand and moved away. Yet the undeniable truth lingered, lengthened into a realisation she'd be a fool to ignore or misinterpret. Cal was emotionally involved in this baby. And in that flash of intimacy, she knew without hesitation that she wanted—*ached*—for him to kiss her.

She dragged in a breath, rough shards of frustration, before stepping back. "It's late. I should…"

"Yes."

Still he just stood there, filling the doorway until she was forced to meet his eyes again.

"Excuse me."

Through the haze of conflicting emotion Cal finally registered her questioning eyes. When he silently moved aside, she brushed past him, the warmth of her body drifting by on a wave of tantalizing perfume. Captivated by her gently swaying hips as she crossed the lounge room, his eyes lingered long after she disappeared into his spare room and shut the door with a decisive click.

He cursed softly, still rooted to the spot. If reality mirrored fantasy, she'd be pulling him towards the bedroom, begging him to make love to her just about now. Instead, he was left with a raw taste in his mouth, a small fire burning a hole in his gut.

With a growl, he stalked out the kitchen, through the living room and down the hall. When he reached his bedroom he began to unbutton his shirt, cursing under his breath when the buttons stuck and he ended up ripping one free.

Ava Reilly was no innocent—she knew exactly what she was doing, from her gentle charming of his mother to the steady gaze she'd given Victor when they'd been introduced. But then this…this pure wonder would practically shine from deep within her and knock him for a six.

Trust your first impressions, Cal, Victor had told him the first day he had started work at VP Tech. *They're there for a reason.*

Grudgingly he had to admit that over the years, Victor had been right on that one. Apart from making his mouth water, Ava had an air of charming, almost old-world innocence. A far cry from the decadent things they'd done weeks ago in his bed. Things he still wanted to do.

What, a small voice rationalized, *if she wasn't pretending?* What if their night together had been as mind-blowing as he'd remembered?

With a swift jerk he pulled his shirt free of his pants.

All his ideas on how to prove—or disprove—his theory involved various stages of getting Ava naked. Something she'd no doubt object to, given her current frame of mind.

Pity.

Five

Ava blinked awake in the darkness, the unfamiliarity panicking her for one second before realization crashed in. She was in Sydney, in Cal's apartment. Today she'd be his official wife-to-be.

With a groan, she reached for her phone to check the time. Five-thirty. If she were home, she'd already be heading outside to watch the sunrise, coffee in hand.

She flung off the sheets and shoved her feet into her sheepskin slippers. Just because she was suddenly living someone else's life didn't mean she should drop her early morning ritual. Yet when she opened the bedroom door into the darkened living room, surprise gave her pause.

Where was the nausea? The morning sickness? She

ran through a mental checklist. Aching breasts—to be expected. A mild twinge in her lower back—probably the strange bed. But her stomach? Nothing.

Thank you, pregnancy gods. With a small sigh, she padded across the room into the kitchen, the watery aquarium's blue glow sending shards of light across the apartment. After inspecting the cupboards, full of gleaming cookware and barely used crockery, she finally found the cups. She chose an elegant bone china teacup and saucer, decorated with tiny blue flowers and totally out of place in Cal's bold apartment. With smooth efficiency, she turned on the water jug and finished her inspection of the kitchen while the water boiled.

The state of the art coffee machine clicked on with a soft beep and her brows wrinkled. Coffee was out unless Cal used decaf...which she seriously doubted. She scowled at the shiny appliance as if it was the manufacturer's fault her daily cup was suddenly off-limits.

"It's on a timer, not telepathy."

She whirled, picking out Cal's large shape in the muted glow.

"You're up early," she blurted out.

"So are you."

When he stepped into the kitchen Ava swallowed. The sudden desire to smooth down his sleep-rumpled hair, stuck in spikes over his head, forced her fingers into a tight fist behind her back. She wanted to run her hands over that broad, cotton-clad chest, to see if the well-worn T-shirt felt as soft as it looked. Instead she turned back to the counter and busied herself with jiggling her caffeine-free tea bag furiously in the cup.

"We country folk get up at the crack of dawn," she said.

"So do we corporate types."

She glanced up with a smile and to her surprise, Cal returned it. Surprise turned to relief as the tension lightened.

She sniffed the air. "Is that butterscotch?"

"Guilty," he reached past her, way too close, to snag a cup from the cupboard above. The aroma of warm man mingled with coffee had her inhaling sharply. "Java Butterscotch, to be exact. I also have Hawaiian Mocha, Blueberry Morning and Cinnamon Hazelnut. I like the variety," he added defensively at her amusement.

"I bet you keep that Gloria Jean's on the corner in business."

When he chuckled, something hot and intimate sent her body into its own little hum. Yet Ava didn't have time to savour the warmth, the delicious anticipation, because following on its heels came a familiar well of nausea.

No! With a quick swallow of her now-tasteless tea, she nodded to the patio. "I'm going to sit out on the balcony."

Cal watched her pad across his lounge room. Dressed in a neatly knotted, fluffy red robe and a pair of absurd slippers, her hair in curly disarray down her back, she couldn't have turned him on more if she'd greeted him in black satin lingerie.

Remembrance assailed his senses, the hint of floral scent innocent yet paradoxically seductive. He knew exactly how that hair felt between his fingers, across his skin, and couldn't stop a small curse escaping as the tangle of memories sparked in his brain.

With his coffee poured, he made his way to the balcony. Yet when he saw her profile, cup raised to her lips, something gave him pause.

He must have made a sound, caught the corner of her vision. She whipped her head around, her shadowed eyes landing squarely on him at the exact moment the sun speared across the balcony. Glints of gold crowned her, a radiant halo for her soft lush features. But it was the expression in her eyes that sent shards of desire straight into his manhood.

Her study of him was intensely personal. Arousing. He felt the burn of her gaze as if she'd run a slow hand over his body, leaving tiny flames in her wake. Her eyes roamed leisurely, first across his shoulders, then his chest. He remained frozen in her commanding grip, taking perverse enjoyment in her unabashed exploration, a hint of a smile kinking the corner of her mouth. Then her eyes dipped lower, much lower, and he instantly hardened.

In a blink her eyes flew to his, full of stricken mortification, before she whipped her head back to the view.

And damn, if he didn't take that as a challenge.

He slid the door open and the gentle warmth of the patio heater rushed him.

Her nose twitched and she suddenly turned, eyeing his cup like it was a redback spider. "Can you...not...?"

"Drink coffee?" He took a sip, smiling.

She swallowed thickly. "The smell…I was fine a moment ago but now…"

"Morning sickness?" His smile fell as she nodded, her eyes panicky as she took another convulsive swallow. Her vulnerability chased away the gentle teasing on his tongue. Swiftly he placed the cup on the floor behind him, then closed the patio doors on it.

She took a ragged sigh. "Thanks. I'm a coffee drinker but apparently this baby hates it."

Cal automatically glanced to her waist, then back to her face. The soft morning light still bathed her, lingering on the tinge of shimmer in her curls. Seeing her this way, devoid of makeup and fancy clothes, a blush still evident on her cheeks, she truly was beautiful. Not like the over-sexual, half-dressed bodies the media portrayed as "perfect," or the expensive, skinny socialites who frequented the few glittery events he'd reluctantly attended. No, Ava's beauty was subtle and seductive, a hint of innocence in those blue eyes, combined with a lush mouth that tilted like a siren's call at the edges.

He remembered her smile, the way her throaty laugh had taken hold of his libido and squeezed.

"What?" she asked curiously, breaking his dangerous train of thought.

With ever-decreasing efficiency he reined himself in. "I'll be home at seven with the papers for you to sign."

Had he just imagined her flinch? It had come out

harsher than he'd intended but when she merely nodded in acknowledgement, he mentally shrugged it off.

"Have a good time today, Ava," he added softly before reopening the patio door, scooping up his cup and leaving her there.

Wrestling his body into submission took longer than expected, but subdue it he did. When he finally left the apartment a half hour later, he'd dressed with a lot less care than he usually reserved for his morning ritual, aided by the tingling recollection of Ava's perusal. The now-familiar irritation of being unable to switch off his thoughts put him in a bad mood for the rest of the day, flaring up whenever he was alone with only memories for company.

Finally, at 7:00 p.m., after a long, frustrating day of meetings, product reports and several cryptic messages from Victor which he'd ignored, Cal stalked into his apartment with precious little patience left.

A wall of delicious aromas slammed into him, stopping him dead. Garlic. He sniffed experimentally as his mouth began to water. Tomatoes, frying meat. He tossed his briefcase on the couch and walked into the kitchen.

The sight of Ava, barefoot in jeans, sweater and an apron, humming a melody as she stirred something in a simmering pot on his cooktop, speared him on a primitive level.

My woman. Mine.

It churned up emotion so surprising, so intense that

it slammed the breath from his lungs. The cliché—barefoot and pregnant, in his kitchen no less—no longer seemed amusing. Because when she threw him a smile and said, "Dinner's ready in five minutes," he wanted nothing more than to drag her into his bed.

"You didn't have to cook." His words came out sharp, borne from frustration and his apparent lack of control.

"I like to cook," she said calmly, her attention resolutely on the pot. "If you don't want it, you don't have to eat it."

Swallowing his retort, he sighted the groceries on the kitchen bench. "Did you order that in?"

She gave him an odd look. "No, I went to the supermarket."

"Did you carry all this?"

She rolled her eyes at the dark suspicion in his voice. "No. Your mother pushed the cart then your doorman delivered it upstairs."

"I thought you went clothes shopping."

"We did." When she offered him a platter of carrot sticks, he took one, crunching it thoughtfully. "You also needed food in your fridge."

"I have food."

"Wine, water, juice, coffee, cereal." She ticked the items off on her fingers. "No fruit, meat, dairy or vegetables."

She turned back to the pot and gave the sauce another stir, but when he remained silent she threw a look over her shoulder. "What?"

He shoved down a myriad of conflicting thoughts, smoothing his expression. "How's the nausea?"

She handed him a knife with a smile. "Gone until the morning, I suspect. Make yourself useful and cut the feta?"

At his round dining table they ate in silence, an odd half tense, half expectant silence. Cal was fully aware of every move, every sound as they devoured the spaghetti and Greek salad she'd made. The tiny scrape of fork on plate, the gentle swallow of water being sipped only amplified the quiet. When he spoke, it was like a shot.

"What did you buy today?"

She downed her fork with deliberate care. "Yes."

Cal eyed her well-worn attire but said nothing.

"A few dresses," she said stiffly. "Some jeans, shoes, skirts. A few tops and a jacket. Don't worry," she added in a small voice. "I won't embarrass you."

Damn. He'd hurt her but didn't know how to fix it, so he did the only thing he could. He let silence do the mending.

"We've had some interview requests," he finally said, placing the cutlery across his plate.

She sat back in her chair, digesting that information. "Do you expect me to give interviews?"

He shrugged. "Only if you want. There's also a bunch of glossies angling for a spread—*Vogue, Elle, Cosmo,* for starters."

"Fashion shoots." She shook her head. "That's just…surreal."

"You're now a news item. You're in demand."

"But only as your fiancée," she countered.

"I thought," Cal said slowly, "women liked getting pampered, dressed up and photographed."

"I don't do 'pampered and dressed up.'" She stood abruptly. "I'm practical, a simple country girl who wears jeans and steel-capped boots. I clean the kitchen, I cook, I wash up. I work with dirt and dig a veggie patch." In quick jerky movements, she began to clear the table. "I'm not glamorous, I'm not model material...I...I have crow's feet and dry heels!"

Her delivery was so frustratingly honest that Cal swallowed his snort of amusement. He couldn't tell if she was simply explaining herself or warning him off.

"So doing girly things scares you."

She shot him a look that lacked venom. "I didn't say that."

"Why not give it a go? You might like it."

"Do you think I might also like some interviewer digging around in my personal life for a couple of hours?"

"That," he returned, following her into the kitchen with his plate, "is where my press office comes in. I can prep you." Decision made, Cal rinsed his plate.

Needing movement, Ava wiped the sparkling benches while he stacked the dishwasher. But when everything had been cleared, tidied and returned to its drawer or shelf, there was nothing left to occupy her hands.

"Go sit outside," Cal said as he reached for the cupboard. "I'll bring you some tea."

Once alone on the balcony, the rigid composure she'd been battling drained. The warmth of the patio heater brushed her skin, a delicious contrast to the sharp bite of cold wind. She grabbed up the throw rug and wrapped it around her shoulders, tucking her feet beneath her bottom as she sat.

Like Alice down the rabbit hole, everything had changed. Gone was peace and quiet, replaced by the shiny boldness of newly acquired fame and fortune. Over lunch at a North Shore café, Isabelle had bluntly described what to expect leading up to the wedding.

"You'll be on everyone's invitation list," the older woman said in between bites of her smoked salmon sandwich. "Parties, social appearances. Requests for fashion shoots and interviews. That's the upside. The downside is less delightful but just as important."

"Rumor and innuendo?"

At Isabelle's serious nod, Ava's smile had dropped. "Yes. Imagine your worst doubts, your deepest fears plastered on the front page of every newspaper in the country. If there's anything you've ever done but don't want the press to know, they'll find it." She leaned back, fixing Ava with a steady look. "It's how you handle it that matters."

Ava shuddered. It was one thing to think the worst of herself, to harbor that black cloud of failure, but to have her insecurities publicly aired for everyone to see?

That was not going to happen.

The moment was broken by the door swooshing open. Cal stepped outside with two steaming cups and a sheaf of papers.

The contract.

He placed it and a pen in front of her, then the cup. With outward calm, she picked up the papers and flicked through them. He'd efficiently tagged the places for her signature but instead of blindly signing, she tucked them beside her on the couch. "I'll have to read this over."

He nodded, settling in the one-seater across from her, a casual version of the previous night. "Of course."

Ava snagged her cup and for a few minutes they remained silent. She'd never felt the need to fill a lull with inane chat, but Cal's presence made her acutely aware of her own, the way she looked, dressed, acted. He made her as nervous as a teenager on her first date.

"Your mother loves to shop," Ava ventured lamely.

"My mother believes shopping is a great icebreaker." He smiled, shifting his large bulk more comfortably in the seat. "It's her great people leveler."

"We *did* talk a lot."

"About?"

"Mostly me. The wedding." She deliberately omitted the topic of Cal's childhood, unwilling to betray Isabelle's generous openness. "I had no idea there were so many bridal magazines on the market."

He couldn't hide a wry grin. "I always suspected Mum was a closet wedding freak. Sorry."

"I don't mind," Ava said truthfully. The woman's enthusiasm had been appealing when she'd gifted her with a bunch of current bridal magazines in the car. *Cosmopolitan Bride, Vogue Bride, Australian Bridal Direc-*

tory, The Bride's Diary…the sheer volume of what Ava had assumed was a narrow topic made her head spin. At first it had taken all her acting skills, pitiful as they were, to smile and thank her for the gift. But Isabelle had sensed her less than enthusiastic response and had clamped a lid on her excitement, instead changing the topic to their day ahead.

And as the day passed, Ava had managed to banish the heavy reality that had settled like cement in her chest and instead found herself enjoying the outing. The subversive shine of the city had already begun to leach in, the bustle and movement exciting her in a way she'd not felt in ages.

"We have two formal functions Thursday and Friday night," Cal said, bringing her back to the present. "I assume those dresses you bought are appropriate?"

She took exception at his tone. "Cal, I'm not completely clueless. I *do* know how to dress."

"Yes." His eyes ran over her, warming her more thoroughly than the tea ever could. "I believe you do." Then he glanced away. "It'll be your first public appearance as my fiancée, so be prepared. There'll be cameras, as well as questions."

"What kind of questions?"

"Ones you'll be expected to know as my fiancée."

"Like what?"

"Well, what would you want to know?"

That threw her for a second and she scrambled. "Umm…why don't you have a computer at home?"

He shook his head. "Don't need one when I have this." He pulled the phone from his pocket and handed it to her. "The new V-Fone. It's a computer, scheduler, GPS and phone in one, all operating with One-Click software. It integrates with my work computer so I'm always contactable. We've had a one-hundred-percent customer satisfaction rating since its launch three months ago."

She ran her hand over the smooth, cold surface, marvelling at the power in such a tiny device, before handing it back. "What are your working hours like?"

He made an offhand gesture. "Long and filled with meetings, budget reports, investment strategies."

"Do you like what you do?"

"I get to travel the world and make million-dollar decisions."

"But do you *like* it?" She probed. "I'm assuming one day you'll be doing Victor's job. That's pretty different than developing software."

His smile was brief and humourless. "I've worked damn hard to earn the right. VP Tech has been my goal since I was seventeen."

"I see." He still hadn't answered her. And was it her imagination or did she sense hesitation in that smooth reply?

"I work twelve- to fourteen-hour days, Monday to Saturday," he added, almost as if trying to justify his non-answer.

"Not Sunday?"

"Sundays are for…relaxing."

She flushed at the deep timbre of his voice. "What's your favourite meal?"

"Lamb roast." The muscles in his face relaxed. "My turn." He paused, assessing her, and for a moment Ava's insides twisted at his complete and utter focus.

"What is…" he paused, "your favourite childhood movie?"

Her mouth tilted. "*The Sound of Music.* Yours?"

"*The Great Escape.* What did you want to be when you grew up?"

"A ballerina—but I wasn't skinny enough."

His eyes grazed her and even beneath the throw rug, she felt her body leap in response. "You look perfectly fine to me."

He was flirting with her. But why? He'd made it perfectly clear she wasn't to be trusted, yet here he was, handing out little snippets of his inner self like party favours. It wasn't in her to question why the sudden good fortune. She just went with the flow.

As the hour ticked by into the next, they shared personal likes and dislikes—he liked action movies, she romantic comedies, they both hated cabbage and pumpkin but loved tropical fruit. After retouching on Cal's career highlights, they landed on the topic of exes.

"I've dated, no one serious," Cal said, swirling the dregs of coffee around in his mug.

"Your mother mentioned Melissa…" She paused at his sharp look.

"What did she say?"

"Just that you were engaged but called it off."

"I see." He placed his cup on the table and leaned forward, elbows resting on his knees. His face became stony and she wondered what the other woman had done to make him so defensive. "And what about you?"

Ava shrugged. "A boyfriend in high school, a couple more when I was working in Jillian's coffee shop. Since I moved back home there's been no one. Gum Tree Falls isn't exactly teeming with eligible bachelors, not like…" She snapped off, too late.

"Like Sydney."

When his eyes narrowed, she could've kicked herself. *That's a record for you, Ava. Undoing all that good work in two seconds flat.*

Cal did not trust her. The sooner she realized that, the easier this would be. Yet pride couldn't let her escape without clearing this ridiculous preconception.

"I came to Sydney for a girlfriend's birthday," she said stiffly. "It was my first time in the city. We had dinner at the Shangri-La then went on to their cocktail lounge. I wasn't looking for a boyfriend or a one-night stand or anything else that night."

"But you found me."

She rose, her face warm. "You approached *me*."

"True. But you didn't say no."

Cal watched the way her face flushed as she threw off the rug then folded it with swift efficiency.

"So now it's a crime to be flattered by a man's attentions? I just wanted one weekend, *one night* to forget about the money, the pressure, the responsibility. For one night I wasn't Will Reilly's daughter, the disappointment, the screwup. The reason for—" She bit off the rest of that sentence, as if realizing she'd said too much. Her eyes, panicky and wide, met his for one fleeting moment, then away.

"It's late," she finally mumbled, refusing to meet his gaze as she reached for the door. "I'm off to bed."

"Ava."

His command fell on deaf ears because with one small click, he was suddenly alone.

Cal remained still for what felt like hours, although his sleek Urwerk watch indicated only minutes. When he'd caught her in that slip there'd been indignation, and hurt. Could she be that good an actress?

Reluctantly, he cast his mind back to that night at the bar, searching through the events to shed some light on his confusion.

At first she'd been wary, even suspicious. His smooth offer to buy her a drink had been met with reluctant acceptance. As they'd shared flirtatious but cryptic details about themselves, she'd gradually warmed to him, enough to have her willing and eager in his bed.

For one crazy second, he let himself indulge in the remembrance of her smile that tilted her mouth into kissable curves, her husky feminine laugh.

What the hell was he supposed to believe?

With a low curse he sprung to his feet and slammed

back inside. The cool shower didn't bring clarity, nor did lying in bed, staring at the LED clock hands as it ticked off the minutes until sunrise.

Six

At one-thirty the next afternoon, Cal braked his car with an irritated yank out the front of his apartment building. He may have stopped grilling Victor about this marriage ultimatum but the man wasn't off the hook yet. Throughout their mid-morning meeting Cal had been icily distant, and as a result the other board members had picked up on the tension. Yet afterwards, instead of calling him on it, Victor had left as swiftly as he'd arrived.

Dammit. With a grunt, he rubbed his temples then glared across at the double glass doors. His normally austere doorman was chatting with a gorgeous dark-haired woman, the old Scotsman sporting a look of rapt adoration on his weathered face.

Then Ava glanced across and spotted him.

All thoughts fled as last night came crashing back, rolling waves breaching his temporary sandbank.

If he'd been enthralled yesterday in the early morning light, now he was riveted. Like some slow-motion teen-age movie close-up, the afternoon sun captured her in its singular glow as she walked out to greet him. She looked like every man's fantasy, from the toes of her black knee-high boots up past the flippy hem of the black skirt barely grazing her knees to the scooped neck of her clingy black sweater. A bright sky-blue trench coat flapped loosely like she'd just flashed someone and her hair bounced over her shoulders in twin shiny black waves, catching the sunlight in raven glints.

His throat went dry, his mouth curving into an auto-matic smile until he caught sight of an expensively suited man unashamedly eyeing her butt as she walked past. A fierce bolt of ownership surged up, ending in a possessive growl as he glared at the man. The starer merely shrugged, smiled apologetically and kept right on walking.

Ava's glossy smile curved shyly as she reached for the door handle. "Hi."

"Hi, yourself." Even with eyes hidden behind fash-ionably round sunglasses, he sensed the unease as she buckled up. "You look…"

"Acceptable?"

"Gorgeous." Cal checked his rear vision mirror, barely catching her flush. "You should dress like that more often."

"Unfortunately, Jindalee isn't too kind on dresses and suede."

"Then it's a good thing we're in Sydney until the weekend. Give those jeans and steel-capped boots a breather."

Her cautious laugh warmed him and they grinned at each other, staying that way for seconds too long, too long to maintain the neutrality of the mood. Cal finally broke the moment, swiftly glancing back over his shoulder before pulling into the traffic.

Ava held her breath, unwilling to break this fragile truce. The man not only developed powerful computer programs, his mind *was* a computer. No doubt he remembered every detail of their conversations, every word both spoken and implied. Yet as Cal shifted gears and the car smoothly eased into second, her jangling nerves began to relax. It was a calming flipside to the last few days' hostility and distrust.

Ava didn't believe in blind optimism, but when she turned her face towards the warm sunshine as they sped across the Harbour Bridge, hope began to spark deep inside. It was…encouraging.

"Based on what you've told me, your due date is the ninth of January." Dr. Wong smiled as he lifted the wand from Ava's stomach. "We can usually tell the baby's sex from about eighteen weeks." He paused, turned a few buttons on the foetal monitor and then pointed to the screen. "Right now, we're just ensuring everything's on track and the baby's forming at the correct rate. There you go."

The exam room was deathly silent, the cool air-conditioned cavern punctuated only by the tiny bleeps and clicks as Dr. Wong took stills from the monitor.

"Just look at that," Ava finally breathed.

Cal remained transfixed on the monitor, at the grey and white snow that indicated a tiny life grew within Ava's belly. He hardly heard the doctor's murmur, the soft snick of the door as the man gave them a private moment alone. His heart was beating way too hard, his blood pounding through every vein in his chest.

Come the new year, he'd be a father. An unexpected flash of something so big, so powerful jumped him from the shadows and left him floundering under the weight. Blindly, he glanced down and Ava's eyes, full of wonder and amazement, undid him all over again.

She was lying on the table, half-covered in a sheet, her skirt rucked up high beneath her breasts. And below that, the soft white skin of her belly, the gentle curve almost imperceptible. He was drawn to her, almost as if he couldn't help himself. It felt natural, right, that he bend down and cover her trembling mouth in a gentle kiss.

And the oddest thing happened. Everything stuttered to a halt.

It seemed like the world had stopped for one amazing second. Ava's breath caught in her throat, astonishment rendering her limbs immobile, until she felt her eyes close, her limbs languidly relaxing into the tender kiss.

Cal had kissed her with bruising urgency before, with uncontrollable passion specifically designed to arouse. But this…this…soft pressure of his warm mouth on hers, almost loving in its gentleness, tightened something deep within until she felt the telltale prick of tears behind her lids.

She barely had time to breathe in the scent of leather, shaving cream and coffee that was so uniquely Cal before it was over, too soon. When he drew back, her eyes flew open, a tiny sound of disappointment rattling in her throat. "Cal…"

His answer was throaty and hoarse. "If you want me to apologise for that—"

"No." She shook her head. "No. It was—" *Amazing. Wonderful.* "—fine."

In the cool, sterile room, she was acutely aware of her semi-nakedness, of her uncovered belly, still wet with the remnants of the ultrasound gel. "Can you pass me a paper towel?"

As if grateful for movement, he turned to the dispenser, grabbed a few towels and handed them over. "I'll wait for you in the lounge." He swiftly pulled out his mobile and in record time was out the door.

Ava frowned. One minute he'd been kissing her, the next he was gone. It was like flicking off a switch, the way he could tease her emotions into tentative expectation then firmly close the door in her face.

With a sigh she finished cleaning up, straightened her clothes and scooped up the pictures the doctor had printed out. The damnable truth was she wanted him to kiss her, wanted him to touch her. Wanted him to ease the aching throb in her body and make sweet love to her.

She opened the door, silently watching Cal as he clicked through his messages. He didn't trust her, they both knew that. Yet she couldn't stop herself wanting him. And therein lay the paradox—how could she want a man who didn't want *her*?

The riddle stuck in her brain for the rest of the day, until she finally forced it away while making cheese-and-pickle sandwiches for dinner.

"Don't cook tonight," Cal had said after he'd dropped her back at his apartment. "I'll be late, so I'll grab something on the way home."

It didn't take a genius to work out the subtext. Ava speared the pickle with vicious intent. *Don't get too comfortable, and don't expect to play happy families.* Well, she wouldn't. For the best part of the afternoon she'd moped around the apartment until her lower back had demanded movement and she'd finally turned off Oprah. Dressed in a blue designer tracksuit that Isabelle had declared matched her eyes, she'd gone for a walk.

The massive spread of suburbia, concrete and noise still overwhelmed and she quickly bypassed the white majesty of the Opera House and headed for the Botanical Gardens instead. For an hour she strolled the lush green lawns and abundant flora until it became clear her presence had attracted unwanted attention.

Being surreptitiously pointed out in loud whispers,

followed by the click of cell phones, was a novelty she didn't care to repeat. Now, as she sat on the balcony and bit into the sandwich, the sharp tang of pickle juice jolted her taste buds. It shouldn't matter that she was low on Cal's priorities, yet it still didn't stop her insides from twisting. He was a businessman and had made an offer based on pure business.

But a child wasn't a business deal.

The sandwich churned in her stomach and she dropped it back on the plate. She may not be top on his list, but instinct told her this baby was. Even if Cal didn't realize it, his reaction at the doctor's gave her hope. It meant that it was a start, however tiny.

It was Saturday night and Ava ignored the throbbing ache in her high-heeled feet and instead pasted a smile on her subtly made-up face. Last night it was a charity event, tonight a glitzy book launch. Two completely different causes yet identical undercurrents, identical partygoers. Decked out in jewels and couture, the women were mostly blond, always tanned and perennially skinny, despite the champagne many downed like seasoned drinkers. The men were expensively attired, oozing privileged wealth and indulgence.

On Cal's arm, Ava felt like the new guppy in the fishbowl, a thousand curious eyes directly squarely on her. Their curiosity had taken many guises—some disbelief, some barely hidden animosity. A few, like tonight's guest of honor, had expressed actual happiness and like a much-needed gulp of water to her drought-stricken mouth, she'd returned the congratulations with genuine warmth.

"You need to do more of that," Cal murmured, a soft rumble in her ear that sent quivers across her skin.

"What?"

"Smile more."

"I am," she replied tightly, her smile still firmly in place.

Cal rolled his eyes. "Now it just looks like you ate a bad prawn."

She snorted out a laugh, one quickly engulfed in the buzz of the fast-growing crowd.

"I can tell you're faking, even if everyone else is fooled," Cal added, his mouth close to her ear. She could feel his warm breath on her sensitive flesh and she clamped down on her bottom lip, stifling a groan.

"I've been to more parties this last week than in my whole life, not to mention the primping and preening and smiling at complete strangers," she muttered back. Many of whom were shallow, appearance-obsessed and way too interested in her cleavage, she realized with a sinking stomach. "And my feet hurt," she added for good measure.

"Do you need to sit?"

Contrition gnawed as she caught the flash of concern on his face. "No," she sighed. Her head still whirled from the million congratulations and curious questions about how and when they met, to the inevitable wedding day. If she heard one more barely dressed woman coyly ask Cal, "When's the big day?" while pointedly ignoring her, she was going to scream.

"Congratulations, Cal. Have you set a date?"

Through the fabric of his Italian suit, Cal felt Ava stiffen, her fingers tightening imperceptibly on his arm. Her face, however, creased into politeness as he introduced the two women.

"Charmed, sweetie." Shannon Curtis-Stein smiled insincerely, her tanned ice-blond figure poured into a black flapper-style dress. Although, Cal conceded, the plunging neckline was hardly in keeping with the era.

Next to all these sleek peacocks, parading their finery and gym-honed bodies with utter confidence, Ava was a breath of fresh air. There'd been a moment when they'd walked into the Hilton's function room and she'd hesitated, staring at the assembled throng as panic skittered across her face. As usual, the women were wearing variations of a familiar theme—short clingy dresses with shoestring straps that showed heaps of leg or toned, muscular backs. Sometimes both. In comparison, Ava's long, floaty strapless silver gown was distinctly elegant. Regal, even. Ignoring the buzz under his skin that had become second nature whenever Ava was around, he'd linked his hand in hers and gave it a reassuring squeeze. And when she'd met his eyes with jaw set, clear blue eyes serious, he knew she wasn't going to buckle.

That's my girl.

He started. Where the hell had that come from? Admiration, yeah, okay. Facing this crowd was a daunting prospect for anyone, let alone a girl from the bush. But laying claim like she was something to own, something exclusively his when they both knew the real truth?

She glanced up at him now and gave him that familiar smile, a shy lip-tilt full of barely hidden apprehension. Even with her body ramrod straight, shoulders back, that smile gave her away every time.

This wasn't a woman in control—she was petrified.

Her hand tightened in his, her breath whooshing out as she breathed deeply. She was way out of her depth, and she knew it. How the hell had he missed that? Her eyes revealed more than she realized from the deep, burning anger at his demands to the desperate control when she'd faced Victor.

It had taken days to realize she couldn't hide her emotions any more than he could stop himself from touching her.

And just like that, his mind cleared. Man, he could stare at her for hours, the way her bare shoulders curved, the elegant sweep of her neck, displayed by her hair piled high. Under his scrutiny, a wayward curl fell, brushing her shoulder in a gentle, teasing kiss.

"You need a necklace to complement your dress," he murmured. "Something that would sit just about—" he drew his fingers sensuously across her collarbone and she gasped "—here."

He paused, his palm a brand on her warm décolletage, unashamedly laying claim. A satisfied smile tugged at his mouth as her eyes widened and her heartbeat upped tempo beneath his hand.

He leaned in, propelled by a desperate urge to follow his hand's path, barely registering Shannon's derisive snort and departure in a whirl of expensive perfume. If he remembered correctly, Ava made the most erotic sound when he licked that sensitive flesh…

She shifted back, a small protest quelling his intent, bringing him back to the present. The noise from the party hit him full-on, as if he'd spent the past few minutes in a sound void and someone had just cranked up the volume.

"What do you think?" He recovered swiftly, only slightly annoyed by the huskiness in his voice.

"I think I feel like an overfed, ruffled sparrow."

At his confusion, she added with a small gesture to the crowd, "Not enough gloss, not enough sophistication."

"You're kidding, right?"

She looked irritated. "No. These women are all perfect. Perfect straight hair, perfect bodies, perfect smiles."

At a loss, he captured her arms and firmly turned her to face him, her back to the crowd. "Name one."

"Lisette Warner," she returned without hesitation.

"She cheats on her husband."

Ava's eyes widened. "Joy Falkner."

"Shallow and bitchy."

"Shannon Curtis-Stein."

"Oh, that's obvious. She's had a boob job."

Her mouth tweaked. "I thought men liked boobs."

"I don't know about 'men,' but fake doesn't do it for me." He couldn't stop himself from eyeing her neckline, modest by the crowd's standards but still affording him a gentle swelling tease of her creamy flesh.

Memory flashed. He recalled the familiar softness of her skin, the way it tasted beneath his hands, his mouth. He didn't have to close his eyes to picture the way her nipples had puckered as he'd gently sucked on them— and as he stared, he saw the imperceptible outline of them now, tightening beneath the snug satin of her dress.

Good Lord. He snapped his eyes up, barely catching her flush of embarrassment before she offered him her profile.

"Trust me, Ava, elegance and style beat skin and bleach every time. Not that there's anything wrong with a little skin…" his voice dipped lower as he leaned in, his mouth temptingly close to her ear, "at the right time."

She slid him a glance, her eyes wide and dark, pupils dilated. Then in the next second, she looked away, her soft breathy intake confirming his suspicion.

He knew arousal when he saw it. Hell, he could practically smell it on her, above and beyond that now-familiar innocent/seductive fragrance she always wore. Despite the thousand reasons why he'd convinced himself to keep his distance, his body began to throb in earnest.

He'd set the boundaries of their relationship and Ava had agreed, so when had the chains of that restriction begun to chafe? Last night he'd had to stop himself from testing the softness of her hair, had paused halfway to place his hand on her belly, a belly that had gently rounded in the past few days. That doctor's appointment had only exacerbated his awareness of his baby growing inside her.

He'd been hell-bent on keeping a physical distance, yet like every big mistake, his downfall had started out small. Last night, as they'd walked into their first official event as an engaged couple, she'd tentatively linked her fingers in his and the blast of guilty pleasure had staggered him. A touch reluctantly given, yet initiated in a moment of desperation, to give her courage. A touch more intimate than a kiss. Her vulnerability simultaneously humbled and aroused him.

So he'd tested his boundaries as they'd mingled with the cream of Sydney society, waiting for her withdrawal as he'd stroked her arm, played with the hair at her nape. She'd jumped the first few times, surprise reflected in her eyes, but eventually that had melted into acceptance. Even welcome, judging by her body's response.

He snaked his arm around her waist now, bringing her hip firmly against him as his hand gently cupped her elbow.

"Cal…"

"What?" He briefly glanced across the room before coming back to her. "We're a happily engaged couple. We're expected to—" he paused, his fingers stroking the sensitive flesh in the crook of her elbow "—touch."

She attempted a laugh, but it came out all shaky and nervous. "You're giving me goosebumps."

He grinned, enjoying her discomfiture way too much. "I hope so. What perfume are you wearing?"

When Cal's voice came, deep and sinful in her ear, Ava trembled.

"Nothing," she managed to croak. "I don't wear perfume."

"Then why," he paused and dipped his head, his jaw barely grazing her neck and sending her eyelids into languid descent, "do you smell so delicious?"

Her body flushed hot, heart kicking hard. "It's called layering…" She ended on a gasp as his murmur of appreciation rumbled over the sensitive spot just below her earlobe. "Body wash," she continued bravely, barely forming the words. "Lotion, body spray. It's…" a sharp intake of breath as his lips gently nibbled on her neck, "Jasmine and peach. Cal, please."

"Mmm?"

She darted her eyes around the crowd. "People are staring."

"No, they're not." His arm tightened around her waist, pinning her to him and she gasped, feeling the evidence of his arousal beneath their clothes.

"Cal," she said firmly, pasting on a gentle smile to appease any casual observers to their exchange. "As much as I appreciate your 'happily engaged couple' act, you really need to stop."

His whole body went completely still.

"I didn't realize you were uncomfortable with my attentions."

And just like that, there was a universe between them.

He may have left his arm around her waist but Ava felt the exact moment he mentally withdrew. The set to his jaw, the cool way his eyes glanced at her then back to the party, made her want to reverse time and take everything back.

She lifted her chin, refusing to let her disappointment show. This was real life, not the movies. He wasn't about to fall desperately in love with her just because she was having his child. If anything, their circumstances only exacerbated distrust, and given what Isabelle had revealed about his past, she didn't really blame him or—

Shock and confusion caught in her throat, rattling around for a few agonising seconds before she slowly exhaled. *No, no way. Cal Prescott didn't fall in love, least of all with someone he didn't trust.*

She eased her weight from one foot then the other, a movement Cal's eagle eyes didn't miss.

"Tired?"

A second ago he'd been aloof, even angry. Now he radiated nothing but solicitousness. A shard of emotion pierced her composure, shocking her. Was she actually *jealous* of her unborn child? It was irrational and shallow but there it was. The baby in her belly—not her—provoked awe, tenderness, concern. She might just as well be an incubator.

"Ava? Are you okay?"

She nodded, unable to speak past the emotion clogging her throat.

"Okaaay." His gaze became unreadable. "Our flight's at eight tomorrow. You want to go home?"

Home. She glanced around the crowded room, at the warm press of strangers laughing, drinking and talking, and felt a pang of homesickness so deep it made her chest ache. "Yes. I want to go home."

He gave her an odd look before placing his hand on her back. "Then let's go."

Seven

The next morning, parked outside VP Tech in Cal's car, a call of nature forced Ava into the foyer in search of a bathroom. His "I'll be a few minutes" was well on its way to fifteen by the time the smiling security guard directed her past the elevators to the restrooms at the far end.

Ava stared at herself in the full-length bathroom mirror. Money shouldn't change who a person was, but right now, seeing this unfamiliar glamorous woman staring back at her, she wasn't so sure. Her hair, usually tied back in a simple ponytail, was now glossy and loose around her shoulders. The faded jeans had been replaced by a long-sleeved shirtdress, the short hem showing off her legs in fashionably high heels. Her face, her skin…she leaned in and blinked under the unforgiving lighting. Her eyes were wider, expertly emphasised with the help of Napoleon Perdis and Isabelle's personal makeup stylist. Her mouth was positively pouty, the rich berry shade matching her dress.

Ava pulled back with a frown. She wasn't Ava Reilly, daughter of William and Bernadette, owner of Jindalee. She was…

"Cal Prescott's fiancée." She paused, then gave an overly bright smile to her reflection. "Hello, I'm Ava Prescott." She took a breath and stepped back. "I'm Mrs. Ava Prescott. Mrs. Ava Reilly-Prescott. Oh, ugh." With a moue of distaste she whirled and shoved the door open with her shoulder.

But just as she was about to round the frosted glass wall, Victor's angry voice pulled her up short.

"You ignore my calls and now you're off back to the bush," Victor was saying, the tinge of derision unmistakable. "The woman's bankrupt. Surely that should tell you something?"

Ava held her breath, cheeks flushing. When Cal spoke, the sharp edges in his clipped reply were unmissable.

"What I do with *my* money is none of your business, Victor."

"But your time is. We have a dozen important meetings coming up this month, not to mention courting those American buyers." Another pause, then Victor added more calmly, "You know your time is money. You can't go jetting off to the back of beyond when you're CEO. It's neither acceptable nor necessary."

"Pot calling the kettle, Victor? You've been absent at least three times in as many weeks."

There was a long, awkward moment. "That's got nothing to do with the company," Victor finally said stiffly.

"And who I'm marrying does?"

That was it. Ava straightened her shoulders, shoved on her sunglasses, then closed the bathroom door with a loud click.

As expected, Victor and Cal had fallen silent when she came into their line of sight. From behind her sunglasses, Ava ignored the thick tension and gave a breezy smile. "Hello, Mr. Prescott," she acknowledged coolly. "How are you?"

"Fine."

For once, his curt reply didn't intimidate her. She'd learned a lot about handling rude people these past few days so instead, she looped her arm around Cal's in casual intimacy. After the debacle of last night, her skin jumped with unexpected joy.

"Bathroom break," she said, holding out his car keys.

Despite the layers of clothing, she felt the unmistakable heat from honed muscle just before his arm bunched beneath her touch. Yet his expression was unreadable, as if he'd shut everything down.

Victor finally spoke. "Take another week to finalize this…project." He barely flicked a glance towards Ava. "But remember VP Tech is your first priority."

"You don't need to remind me about priorities, Victor."

A look passed between the two men but Ava was too disturbed to pay it any attention. *Of course the company was his first priority.* It was a fantasy to think she'd actually pondered giving in to her body's demands, that some time in the last few days she thought Cal had begun to believe she was incapable of the deceit and that they'd had a chance of making this sham marriage work.

She swallowed the throbbing hurt, taking a few seconds to gather her racing thoughts, to smooth her expression into something resembling neutrality.

Victor's gruff voice brought her back to the present.

"Isabelle wants to throw you an engagement party."

Cal grimaced. "I don't have—"

"You're getting married and your mother wants to celebrate it."

Ava felt Cal tense again just before he nodded and turned, steering her towards the door. "Fine. Jenny will let you know what day suits. Now if you'll excuse us? We have a plane to catch."

Two hours later, Ava watched Cal take in Gum Tree Falls, seeing it through his eyes for the first time as they drove through: the single main street in all its unapologetic outback glory, old weather-beaten stores, cracked guttering that flanked the potholed bitumen road. The rolling hills in the distance, covered with native gum trees and bushland scrub, and the grazing sheep that were the lifeblood of the small country town.

Sydney felt like a century away, not just a half-hour flight and twenty minute drive from Parkes, the closest town that could pass for civilisation.

The ties of the past reached in, entwining around her chest, constricting her breath. And suddenly she was seventeen all over again, desperate to escape the chains of her youth. If she closed her eyes now, she could hear the gentle whispers starting up, a thousand buzzing flies swarming in her head.

"What does 'Jindalee' mean?" Cal asked, breaking through her thoughts.

She studied him as he drove, a picture of wealthy, sunglasses-clad confidence at the wheel of this top-of-the-line hire car. "It's Aboriginal for 'one-tree hill.' See?" She pointed to the main house, then the massive gum tree a hundred meters away. "My father built on the one hill he didn't have to deforest."

"He was a conservationist?"

Her mouth twisted as they pulled into Jindalee's parking area. "No. Less labour, therefore, less cost."

Cal said nothing, instead dragging on the handbrake and killing the engine. Last time he'd barely had a chance to notice his surroundings. Now he swung open his door and took a long sweeping look.

From the outside, the homestead fitted every sense of the word—walls made from large slabs and roughly mortared, topped with an olive-green corrugated roof. A wooden porch that ran right around the house. Two large plant pots with wild greenery flanked the wooden steps that led up to massive wooden double doors. A small wrought-iron table and two chairs sat to the left of the entrance; and on the right a wooden loveseat covered in a long, colourful cushion.

As Cal reached in to remove their bags, the doors opened and a small, elderly woman emerged. When he straightened, the woman and Ava were deep in conversation, their heads side by side in comfortable intimacy.

The woman gently swept her hand across Ava's belly and said something, prompting Ava to laugh. That small, simple reaction seemed to relax her body and for one moment, he felt a shot of something race through his chest. Yet when Ava turned to include him in the welcome, he remained rooted to the spot. Since last night the strain between them had been palpable and he was unwilling to exacerbate that by intruding on the moment.

Ava's half curious, half confused frown finally propelled him forward.

"Cal, this is Aunt Jillian."

Jillian's welcoming hug was like being wrapped in a comforting blanket. Like Ava she only came to his shoulder, but the genuine warmth in her embrace shone through, creasing her face into a smile.

"Welcome to Jindalee, Cal. I just wish you had more time to settle in before…" She looked at Ava apologetically. "Sorry, darling. Lord knows how she knew you were coming. I couldn't get her to leave—"

"Don't worry, Aunt Jill." Ava stroked her arm. To Cal

she added, "You're about to get a crash course in small-town curiosity." Then she glanced over his shoulder, pasting on a too-bright smile. "Anne! How are you?"

Cal turned to see a thin, middle-aged woman descend the stairs. Her greying hair was wound up into a wobbling bun as she fast-walked over to them, her long face split wide with a smile.

"Look at you, Ava! All dolled up like some fancy city wife-to-be! I heard you'd gotten yourself engaged to a Sydney man and came to see with my own eyes."

Cal noticed the way Ava suffered the cheek kiss before pointedly pulling back. The woman didn't notice anything amiss though, because she turned to Cal and kept right on talking.

"I'm so thrilled Ava finally managed to find herself a man. I don't have to tell you what a wild little thing she was. Born and raised in the Falls, just like me, but Ava, well, she's been a little cracker from day one. It's kept the whole town entertained, wondering what she'll get up to next!" She paused to laugh, oblivious that she was the only amused one. "Let me see, when she was five, she was bitten by a redback, then the following year, a cattle dog—"

"Anne," interrupted Jillian, but the other woman was on a roll.

"Oh, and skinny dipping in Reilly Dam when she was twelve. Then of course, there was the Dean incident," she added sotto voce, "and let's not even mention—"

"Let's not," Ava said sharply.

Startled, Anne blinked then quickly stuttered, "but you came good in the end!" She beamed, giving Ava a shoulder hug and shaking her firmly for good measure, unaware of Ava's frozen expression. "I'm Anne Flanagan, by the way."

She offered her hand to Cal and he shook it. "Cal Prescott."

"Prescott?" Anne smiled indulgently at Ava. "I read that but thought it was a typo. 'Surely that can't be our Ava,' I said to Jillian. 'Isn't that the name of the VP Tech billionaire?'"

Cal couldn't quite hide a self-satisfied smile. "That's me. Victor Prescott is my father."

For one amused second he thought the woman would faint but Jillian swooped in to take Anne's arm, steering her to her car. "It's nearly nine. Don't you have to open the café?"

"Oh, yes!" Anne fluttered, digging in her purse for her keys. "And after you're both settled in, come on over and I'll fix you up coffee and scones, on the house. No, Ava, I won't take no for an answer!" She opened the car door and beamed at them both. "Fancy that—a billionaire. You did well, Ava! Toodles!"

And then she was gone in a roar of dust.

Cal noticed Jillian had moved back towards the house, giving them privacy. Ava stood stock still, her back to him, facing the now-empty road as dust settled around them, until finally another car crested the rise, destroying the awkward moment.

"Well." Ava suddenly turned. "There's your team. Let's go in and get started, shall we?"

The too-polite smile stretched her mouth wide, emphasising the odd sheen in her eyes before she blinked it away. She looked so alone yet so defiantly rigid that the urge to wrap her in his arms was almost like a physical ache.

"Ava."

"What?" She reached into the hire car and retrieved her handbag, swinging it onto her shoulder before facing him. She just stood there, looking gorgeous and classy in that red dress and black coat, brittle control barely holding her expression together. He recognized the familiar act, the one where you pretend everything's normal even when it was damn well not.

"We'll have to use my office," she said brightly. "No doubt Jillian's already seen to lunch and the tea breaks."

Her gaze held his, challenging him. With an inward sigh, he let it go with a nod.

Yet as she clicked up the front steps, his eyes followed her. He'd get an explanation from her. Later.

They're guests, Ava told herself as Cal and his team followed her down the path to Jindalee's guest houses. *Just guests asking for a tour.* No need to panic, no need to get nervous. She managed to remain calm and professional as she led them through the rooms, the kitchen, the dining area. But when it came time to settle into her office and pick apart just exactly where she'd gone wrong, those butterflies rushed up, fluttering crazily in her chest.

After the meeting paused for lunch, Ava sat in her chair, her brain buzzing from everything they'd discussed. As the others gathered outside to debate the value of the amazing view, she and Cal were alone, the only sound the nervous in-out-in click of the pen beneath her thumb. When he pointedly glanced up from his papers, she flushed and shoved the pen across the table.

Had she actually worried about losing control of the one thing that was still hers? Cal's staff—Judy Neumann, Margie Mason and Jack Portelli—were professional and experienced, from suggesting color schemes and menu changes to creating a larger Internet presence and a membership incentive card.

Her head spun with information overload and, lethargy forgotten, she scraped back her chair, went over to the low filing cabinet and poured herself a glass of juice. Cal had confidently presented this multi-million-dollar overhaul with the bottomless pockets of the Prescott name behind him. His team had enthusiastically gone through the proposal and she'd found herself seduced by their ideas, their energy. And when she'd glanced at Cal, she had been struck by his encouraging nods and satisfied smile at their presentation. He entered discussions but knew when to step back. He made suggestions and then let her make the final decisions. He had a way with his staff that didn't stifle their creativity, didn't step on toes and more importantly, let them take the lead while still maintaining control.

He may be a tech geek, but the man was a natural with people, too.

"What do you think?"

Ava looked up, startled to find Cal standing beside her. "I'm amazed they came up with all this in such a short time. I'm very impressed, but—"

"What?"

"Do you really think marketing Jindalee as an exclusive health spa retreat will work?" She palmed the bottom of her glass, fingers wrapping around the cold condensation. "Wouldn't the rich and famous rather party all night in a big city?"

His mouth quirked. "There are some who're interested in an authentic outback experience."

"With feather canopy beds and spa treatments?"

"Our focus group wants the facade without the gritty reality. At Jindalee they'll be fed, pampered and waited on, with this as their backdrop." He swept his arm wide to encompass the unfettered view from the huge window. Mile upon mile of gently undulating hills backed him up, stark against the bright blue sky. The gum trees swayed as grey storm clouds massed in the far distance, threatening rain.

"But what you're suggesting…" She turned back to the table and picked up the floor plans. "Treatment rooms, mud baths, indoor spa and sauna—it would double Jindalee's size. We'd have to apply for building permits, not to mention shutting the place down for months."

Cal shrugged, unfazed. "The permits aren't a problem, not when we'll be creating local jobs. And it's not as if you're making a profit, so shutting down isn't an issue."

Her face flushed. "It's not just about making a profit, Cal. This place is more than bricks and mortar to me."

With one fluid movement, he crossed his arms and put his shoulder to the wall. His long fingers gently tapped one defined bicep, his expression thoughtful. She could get lost in those eyes—intelligent, assessing eyes that constantly reminded her of the decadent hours they'd shared.

"So let me make Jindalee into something unforgettable," he finally said.

She turned back to the window, placing the forgotten juice on the cabinet. "It's already unforgettable."

"But not profitable, which is what you need."

She frowned, studying her reflection in the tinted glass. "What's it all going to cost?"

"Don't worry." She glanced back and his eyes locked onto hers. "I don't renege on a deal, Ava. I said whatever it takes. This is it."

Before she could say anything further, he straightened and reached for his jacket. "Let's take a break and you can show me the town."

"Tell me I wasn't in the Twilight Zone back there."

Ava gave him a pained look as he guided her back up Jindalee's front steps, his hand a now-familiar warmth on her back. "Welcome to my life."

"They're like a bunch of gossiping high schoolers. Can't they talk about anything else than what you did ten years ago?"

"Like rising feed prices, the continuing drought…. The latest brand of stock whip? Not half as much fun as placing bets on what I'll do to screw up next."

Her footfalls echoed on the decking as she went over to the long wooden bench. Cal recognised the tension pulling at her shoulders as she sank into the cushions with a sigh. She was wound up enough to make his own muscles ache in sympathy. Not the type of person tough enough to play out a ruthless game of blackmail. In fact, if he were completely honest, her whole demeanour under pressure had been contrary to every assumption he'd made.

Irritated, he said shortly, "So why didn't you leave?"

"My father built Jindalee from nothing."

"That's not an answer." He leaned against the porch railing.

She sighed, a deeply troubled sound. "I lived with Jill in Parkes for a few years, working at her café, but I still missed this place. Just look around." She indicated the scenery with the small lift of her chin. "This place is…powerful and humbling. It's extreme—flash storms one day, glorious sunshine the next. It's welcoming, familiar. Beautiful." She fixed her eyes on him, stormy and honest. "Why do I stay? Because of this." Her arm swept out, encompassing everything around them. "It's about the glory of a morning sunrise, when it feels like there's no one else in the world. It's about the tranquillity of a warm summer night. It's something—" she paused, struggling to find the words "—almost spiritual." She gave a small smile. "I'm not very good at describing it, am I?"

"It's about finding peace within the land."

Dumbfounded at his perception, Ava nodded. "That's right. It's about the land, not those people in town."

"So why not give them something positive to talk about? Let me make Jindalee that something, Ava," he added seriously.

Ava swallowed a throbbing heartbeat as her breath caught. The sheer command, the utter confidence in his intense gaze was dangerously hypnotic. *So this is how it feels.* To be rescued. Like she was a fifteenth-century damsel saved from marauding invaders by the powerful, heroic knight.

All she could do was nod again until the threatening rumble of distant thunder forced her gaze skyward.

"It's going to rain." She rose to her feet and reached for the door. Every inch of her skin seemed to tingle as he followed her in, her body leaping to life despite her desperation to ignore it.

If the morning had been a whirlwind of emotion, the rest of the day was torture, like her senses were playing some horrible game of "I told you so." When she looked at Cal, she not only remembered those lips kissing her. Now she recalled the way he'd used his daunting presence to preempt all those nosy questions in town. Staring at the conference table only brought his hands into her eyeline—hands with long, teasing fingers that knew how to touch, stroke. Caress. She couldn't even block him out by focussing out the window because she could still hear that sinful, liquid, caramel-chocolate-honey voice, constantly reminding her of erotic whispers, satisfied sighs.

The meeting finally broke up at six. With Cal finishing up in the office, Ava showed everyone out, shaking their hands with a bright smile and thanking them for their efforts. But the instant she closed the door, exhaustion rushed in.

Cal found her there, sagging into the heavy door with her forehead against the dark wood. Her shoes had been replaced by comfortable slippers, her sleeves were rolled up and her lipstick was long gone. She'd swept her tumble of hair into a sloppy ponytail and it now dragged down her back with a few tendrils loose and curling over her shoulder.

The present suddenly slammed into the past, creating a sharp, aching desire that went straight to his groin. He'd felt her eyes on him all afternoon, as if he were part of some intensive study. Yet when he'd glanced her way, she'd avoided his questioning gaze.

"Are you okay?"

She jerked upright, almost guiltily, before turning to him and smoothing back her hair. "Just tired."

"Then come and sit down."

She looked at his outstretched hand, then quickly back at him as if waiting for the catch. The doubt on her face twisted his gut.

"Come on."

With obvious reluctance, she took his hand. As he folded his fingers around her cold ones, warmth sliced into him.

"Are you hungry?" she asked faintly as he led her down the hall towards the living area. He could feel the pulse beat steadily beneath the delicate skin on her wrist.

"Not really. You?"

She gave him a quick smile. "Starving."

He made a detour and they ended up in the kitchen. Cal pulled out a chair and encouraged her to sit as he opened the fridge.

"You don't have to cook for me. I can—"

"No," he said with a decisive shake of his head. "I think I can manage a microwave."

She smiled back, an innocent response that still succeeded in kicking up his heart rate. "There's soup on the bottom shelf."

Ten minutes later he presented her with hot tomato soup and thick toast before settling in the chair opposite. Since last night he'd begun to recall more things, disturbing things that were contrary to his original assessment of this woman. It wasn't only the inbuilt elegance, the expressive eyes. It was in her tiny, unselfconscious movements, like the way she nervously shoved her hair back, or when she straightened her shoulders in firm determination.

If it was all an act, he should've seen the cracks by now.

"Something's been bugging me."

She paused, the spoon half way to her lips. "About?"

"You."

She flushed and placed the spoon back in the bowl, waiting his next move.

"Tell me about your sister," he finally said. "What was she like?"

Her eyes spilled sudden emotions before she efficiently gathered them back up. "Grace was…" She smiled. "Beautiful. Poised. Well-mannered. She wanted to be a fashion designer, a painter, a vet. She finally settled on psychology, of all things. And she would've been damn good at it, too. She radiated humor and joy. Everyone adored her. She was the good one, the angel."

By her own omission, Cal drew the assumption. "And you weren't."

She stirred her soup absently. "I was her polar opposite."

"You got the blame for her death."

Her eyes snapped to his. "I wasn't charged," she said almost defiantly.

He met her probing stare head-on and a moment later, she nodded, as if coming to an important decision. "The crash was my fault. It was dark and I was speeding."

Underneath her brittle expression he recognised the desperate need to belong, to be accepted for who she was, not defined by what she'd done or who her father had been. With a start, Cal realized that was him at twelve, uprooted from his mediocre life and transported into a different universe where wealth and privilege ruled. Yes, Sydney society had its gossipmongers, but money talked louder. The Prescott name demanded respect. Here they treated Ava like a misfit child, pointing out her screwups under the guise of humour, not allowing her to forget.

Once he'd given a damn what others thought of him, once he'd been desperate for a father figure, to make his own way, to be someone. It stunned him to realize that thanks to Victor's ultimatum he was still trying to prove himself.

"My father stopped speaking to me," she said now. "I lived with Jillian for five years until my mother got sick."

"He kicked you out because of an accident?" He scowled.

"No, he kicked me out two months before when I refused to stop seeing a boy he disliked. The Dean situation," she clarified, crossing her arms on the table. "One day I convinced Grace to sneak out and go shopping. I was driving her back home, it was late and we came across the back paddock after dark. I took a crest too fast and crashed in a ditch."

Ava took a breath, noting the scowl on Cal's face had deepened, but she was too caught up to stop the tumble of words erupting from her mouth. It wasn't the memories that made her sad, it was her inability to change them. But he'd started this conversation and she didn't know how to stop it with anything but the cold hard truth.

"I don't remember anything after slamming my head on the steering wheel." She rubbed her temple, refusing to let those gut-wrenching memories take hold. "But when I woke up in hospital I had a broken arm and Grace was dead."

"And your father cut you from his life."

Ava shook her head. "You have to understand that this was a man who ruled his family with loads of discipline and little emotional reward. He was ex-army, a man who never showed weakness or affection and thought apologies were for sissies. He and I clashed from the very beginning." She gave a small smile. "And I did a lot of things just to piss him off. Grace…" She shook her head. "Grace was the peacemaker. She hated conflict and tried to convince him to talk to me. Then the accident happened and that was it until my mother was diagnosed with cancer."

"He asked you to come home?"

She nodded, the memory of her proud, gruff father brought low and humbled by the uncomfortable reality of her mother's death sentence. "Whatever Dad's faults, he loved Mum. He'd do anything for her and the only thing she wanted was a truce before she died."

The gentle ping of the kitchen clock echoed in the cooling stillness, ticking off the seconds until Ava spoke again.

"Are you sure you're not hungry? Do you want a drink? Coffee?" She smiled wryly. "It's not up to Sydney standards but still pretty good." She rose to her feet but ended up stifling a gasp.

Instantly Cal's hand shot out, grabbing her arm. "What?"

"Pins and needles."

"You need to put your feet up." His command brooked no refusal and Ava was exhausted. She let him lead her into the lounge room, push her gently into a chair and shove an ottoman under her legs.

With a deep sigh, she muttered her thanks, leaned back and closed her eyes.

Eight

Hours later Ava woke with a start. Someone had stoked the fire and it burned away merrily in the darkness. She shifted, noticing for the first time the blanket tucking her in.

"You're awake."

Cal sat on the couch opposite, firelight flickering over his broad shoulders. His shirtsleeves were rolled up, collar and buttons askew where he'd yanked off his tie. Paperwork lay forgotten on the coffee table as he leaned forward, elbows on his knees. Had he been watching her sleep? She felt the flush across her cheeks and shoved the blanket down.

A languorous warmth spread into her legs, making

them tingle as he continued to watch her. It was like he was trying to figure something out but the answer continued to elude him.

"Can you stop that?" she finally said.

"What?"

"Staring at me."

His mouth spread in languid pleasure, causing her to flush again. "You don't like me looking at you?"

"It's disturbing." More than that, it aroused her. She tried to rein in the memories, refuse their hold, but it was like swimming through mud. She swallowed thickly, forcing her breath to even out.

This deep, aching desire was excruciatingly familiar. It had seized her common sense once before, nine weeks ago, when she'd been lulled by a sinful voice and seductive eyes.

She rubbed a hand over her eyes.

"Have you eaten?" she asked.

"Yep."

She dropped her feet to the hardwood floor welcoming the cold shock. "You didn't have to wait up. I can show you to your room if you—"

"Ava," he interrupted, "you don't have to do everything yourself."

Confusion spread across her face but it was the hint of sadness, carefully masked, that drew Cal in. "But I have to."

"Why?"

She hesitated. "Because no one else will."

In the darkened room, the peace broken only by the gentle hiss and crackle from the fire, Cal rose.

"Well…" She shoved her hair back from her face with a tentative smile that didn't quite work. "Good night." He caught her look, vulnerability tinged with steely determination, before she stood and severed eye contact. She looked away as if her feelings were somehow shameful, something to be hidden.

He didn't think, didn't hesitate. He just moved.

When he pulled her into his arms, she stiffened, resisting at first. But she was no match for his insistence. Her small sigh shuddered into him, contracting something buried deep inside his chest.

"I'm not going anywhere," he murmured.

For now. The unspoken truth lay between them, something intangible that still commanded a physical presence. Ava let herself wallow in the moment of weakness. It felt good to be held by a man, to have strong, warm arms wrapped around her. It made the world safe and right, it made her feel protected and loved. She wanted to stay this way forever.

Something shifted inside, something that she couldn't describe. For the first time in forever, she felt like someone else was on her side. She felt championed. Wanted.

Ava couldn't pinpoint the moment everything flipped, only that it did. His embrace was meant to comfort, and for a few moments it did just that, but when she lifted her head from his shoulder something changed. It could've been the way his eyes held hers, dark pools of intense complexity. It could have been her will, desperately tired of the front she'd thrown up against this emotional onslaught.

Whatever the reason, everything shorted out as she tipped her mouth up to his and whispered, "Kiss me."

Her soft words crashed into his mouth, then rolled back on his sharp exhale. She barely had time to regret, rethink, before his groan hit her and his mouth was suddenly covering hers in deep, searing possession.

Sensation collided in her brain, sparking a rush of blood through every secret corner of her body. Her half-groan, half-sigh against his lips only seemed to encourage him, because he angled her mouth to taste deeper, his tongue firmly pushing her lips apart. If it was hormones or just hot-blooded desire, she didn't know. Didn't care. She wrapped her arms around his neck and strained forward, offering herself. When her breasts, now full and throbbing, mashed up against the hard wall of his chest she groaned at the sweet, aching bliss.

It was what she'd wanted, what she'd burned for, ever since he'd turned up on her doorstep.

A low pulse began in the pit of her belly, fanning upwards and heating her skin. He seemed to sense that, because he released her face to skim his hands across her collarbone, then down her arms before coming to rest on her hips.

She shivered, skin prickling with eagerness, desire making her bold. She dragged her hands across his shoulders, then eased her fingers under his sleeves, ending on a sigh when she encountered honed, hot muscle beneath the soft cotton. She kneaded, she stroked. She craved. Like a drug thickening her blood, making her limbs languid, she felt desirable, wanted. And she wanted him.

His flesh beneath her palms sent a myriad of sensations bursting behind her eyes, only to ratchet up higher when he groaned low in her mouth, sending a primeval thrill into every bone. With one swift movement he grabbed her bottom, pulling her sharply up against him, against the hard, throbbing arousal separated by only two thin layers of clothing.

Cal's iron-grip control began to slip. All he could feel were the luscious curves of her butt beneath his hands, her hard nipples digging into his chest like two tiny pebbles. Her amazing scent teased his nostrils, his senses, coupled with the glorious musky sweetness of warm woman.

His blood pulsed quick and hard, threatening to demolish the promise he'd made. Yet like a sudden match sparking in the pitch black, reality flared. He didn't want it, didn't need it, but he couldn't ignore it.

When Cal suddenly broke the kiss, breathing hard, Ava murmured her disappointment. But when she leaned in, seeking the warmth of his mouth again, he tilted away then released her, the way barred. Rejected, she stepped back.

His eyes bored into hers, mysterious and unfathomable. Then he dragged a hand across his chin, the grating rasp of his five o'clock shadow echoing in the dark, intimate silence. "I'm trying, I'm trying to keep my word, but dammit, don't start what you're not going to finish."

That last word came out husky and hoarse and she opened her mouth to protest, but no words came. Instead, with heat flushing her cheeks, she backed away until there was nothing but cold space and air between them.

"I feel…I want…" She paused, her head whirling. It felt like someone had bundled up all her raw emotions, magnified them a thousandfold and was now pegging them back at her. And Cal just stood there, silent, waiting.

She took a deep breath and straightened her shoulders. "The truth is, I have a billion hormones racing around inside me. Morning sickness, fluid retention—" she picked up a lock of hair and it curled around her finger "—even my hair has changed. Yes, I'm attracted to you, but I didn't expect…" *To want you this badly?* How on earth could she admit that?

"I see." Under his slow, excruciating perusal Ava wanted to escape so badly her calves began to tense. "So what do you want to do?"

"I don't know."

Cal nearly groaned aloud. It'd been so long since he'd believed in honesty, in the goodness of someone who didn't demand something in return. If her agonised whisper hadn't got him, the look in her eyes did—eyes normally so clear and wide, now cloudy with confusion.

Cal wasn't a man who denied himself much of anything: if something was offered he went after it. Ava was offering but amazingly, she hadn't convinced herself yet.

With the ache in his jaw echoing the throb in his groin, he gathered up the files and turned for the door, envisioning a long, cold shower.

"Good night, Ava."

"Cal, wait."

Her words washed over him, her gentle plea stroking along his sensitive flesh, stopping him dead. He tried to force his body to settle but all he wanted to do was reach out and finish what they'd started. His skin ached in anticipation, every inch humming in earnest.

"What?"

He turned then, to her flushed face, fingers threading uneasily through her hair. She looked so unsure, so ready to bolt yet so absurdly beautiful that his tongue stuck to the roof of his mouth. And suddenly, everything became clear.

"You know what I think?"

Nervous and still sluggish with passion, Ava could barely get out a whispered, "What?"

"I want you."

She held her breath as he paused, dangling the moment like a tempting prize. "I want you in my bed. Under me." His mouth curved, a sensual sculpture in warm flesh as his voice took on a throbbing, hypnotic rumble.

"Above me," he drew out every syllable for maximum effect, punctuating with measured, predatory steps. "I want to hear you moan, to kiss you…everywhere."

"What—" her voice came in low and rough and just a little bit hoarse "—are you doing?"

"I got fed up waiting for you to ask."

With a low moan she met him in the middle and gave herself up to his mouth. She suffered the bittersweet torture of his lips feathering over hers, testing then tasting her bottom lip while her breath kicked up. It took almost superhuman effort not to plead, to beg him to take her right here, right now.

Cal could feel her tense beneath his hands but focused on the kiss, tenderly sweeping his mouth over to the corners of hers, tracing the edges with his tongue. Even though he knew her body intimately, had kissed every inch of it, they'd never shared a kiss like this. Not something so incredibly gentle that still succeeded in arousing him from go to whoa in seconds flat.

His lips trailed away from her mouth, across the curve of her cheek before ending at her ear.

She gasped, her hot breath skimming across his jaw, making him shudder.

"Where's your room?"

Somehow they made it down the hall, to Ava's bedroom at the back of the house. No sooner had she closed the door behind them than Cal swiftly took control, pushing her up against the wall and mashing her breasts against his chest. Her nipples peaked against his shirt, sending hot, urgent need surging through his body. He grabbed her face and kissed her again.

Ava felt the effects of that mind-numbing kiss explode through her veins. All this time she'd been denying the sinful indulgence of his lips, his mouth, and for what? His arms pinned her but she felt safe. His mouth devoured but she felt wanted. His arousal dug into her stomach, and she felt desirable.

His mouth eased hers open in a deep growl as if the thought of denying him entry was possible. It wasn't. She wanted his mouth, his tongue, his touch. Caught up in the kiss, she nearly jumped out of her skin when he plucked open the buttons of her dress. His hot hands quickly replaced the blast of cold and with a groan she angled her head, opening her mouth wider to his invading tongue.

His instant husky murmur shot white-hot need straight between her legs. She remembered how perfectly they fit. No awkwardness, no fumbling. Just pure poetry in motion, two dancers in unison, following the steps they knew by heart. Their one night together hadn't just been a crazy, larger-than-life event she'd promoted in her mind as the pinnacle of pleasure. It had been everything and more.

She ached to touch him, to feel the texture of his skin, the way it heated beneath her fingers, her mouth, her tongue. Feverishly, she grabbed his shirt, fumbling with the buttons until he took pity on her and just yanked it off.

At first she gasped as the buttons popped, flying

across the room, hitting her dresser with a tiny ping. But then he smiled, a wicked, sensuous smile full of knowledge, one for her and her only, and suddenly, something deep inside burst.

It must have registered in her eyes because he tumbled her to the bed, mouths locked in a renewed bout of frenzied kisses. Quickly her dress came down, pooling around her waist and then his mouth was on her breast, covering one painfully peaked nipple through the satin fabric of her bra.

Sensation exploded through her nerve endings, sending her back arching, her breath gasping. It was intense, unbearable, and she grabbed him, prepared to shove him away, but he preempted her, pinning her hands above her head.

"You like that?"

Ava panted, her eyes wide as she stared up into that sensual smile. "Too much."

His smile widened. "So if I, for example, did this—" he bent and dragged the bra aside with his teeth and she gasped as her nipple sprang free "—then this—" he licked at the tightened bud then blew gently, peaking her tender flesh into almost unbearable hardness "—that wouldn't be good?"

God, that voice. That deep, slow, seductive voice making her limbs melt, promising hours of wicked joy. Ava whimpered, gently rocking her hips, but all that succeeded in doing was settling his hardness more comfortably between her legs.

"You know it's more than good," she whispered, tilting her head back as frustration and arousal raced through her veins. But avoiding his eyes didn't ease her throbbing desire. Instead, Cal's deep, rumbling chuckle flooded over her skin, a second before his mouth covered her nipple.

She bucked, but it was futile. Need roared through her skin, burning, unbearable. Her whole body trembled as his lips and tongue worshipped her flesh, his teeth rasping gently, teasing, peaking. Her eyes snapped down, only to find him studying her, his mouth claiming her breast as he boldly teased her other nipple into hardness with his thumb.

"Cal, please." The plea slipped out but she was past caring anymore. "I need you."

"Wait."

Hot, desperate desire clawed through Cal, burning his body from the inside out. But still he continued his exploration, cupping the new fullness of her breasts before kissing a path between the erotic valley, stroking her warm, fragrant flesh before ringing his tongue around the nipple then taking that rock-hard bud deep in his mouth.

He was enjoying seeing her squirm, caught up in the familiar wave of white-hot passion—until he heard her gasp, followed by a frustrated groan. And suddenly, need bubbled over, scorching him with its intensity.

"Cal…please!"

He clenched his teeth, desperate for control, as he swiftly reached under her dress and dragged her knickers down.

She managed the buttons of his pants, then his zipper, before he stood and yanked his pants and boxers free. Then with a groan he sank back down into Ava's welcoming body.

"Hurry." Her breathy demand echoed in the thick stillness and he needed no further urging.

With one smooth thrust, he parted her legs and buried himself inside her.

Their breaths hissed out in simultaneous wonder, the air congealing around them and meshing with the scent of warm arousal. Then Cal cupped the warm flesh of her bottom and began to move.

They spoke in murmurs and sighs, their rhythm at first hesitant, then growing in familiarity. A glorious wave swept Ava, her entire body humming and hot. Cal was large and a tight fit, but she accommodated him like they were two pieces of the same puzzle. A perfect match.

He'd trapped her hands above her head in a sensuous prison, their fingers linked in fragile intimacy. And when he upped the pace, she threw her head back and gave herself up to him.

Their ragged breathing punctuated the air, mingling as he dipped down to kiss her briefly once, then again. Farther down, between her throbbing legs, she felt the sensuous glide as he filled her, pulled back, then thrust again. He'd been gentle at first, as if testing his welcome, and when she finally dragged open her eyes and focused on his, they were almost black and seriously intent on pleasuring her.

She angled her hips upward and on the next thrust he went deeper. She was rewarded with his groan, which came from the most private places inside, and she murmured her satisfaction.

Cal was nearing the edge, too quick. The need for release clawed inside, sending a wave of sweat beading across his skin. Their bodies were already shiny-slick with it, and when Ava leaned up to nibble gently at his shoulder, he nearly lost it then and there. With a soft command he pushed her back before gritting his teeth and picking up the rhythm.

He sensed just before he felt the buildup of Ava's climax. All around him her tightly wound muscles squeezed and with a groan, he held on to the thin skein of his control, determined to make sure she took pleasure first.

Wait…wait…

Their heartbeats mingled, pounding insistently for precious seconds. And then it happened. Her eyes widened, her breath coming out in tiny, almost amazed gasps, before her warmth flooded him totally, completely. He released the breath he hadn't realized he'd been holding and with relief thrust once, twice.

As Ava gave into the glorious sensations, shudders wracking her body, she felt Cal's hot breath in her ear, his groan as he, too, reached his climax before collapsing, stealing the breath from her body in a deliciously crushing embrace.

She became aware of their breathing, echoing loud and

harsh, as she floated back down to earth. Unwilling to break the afterglow, she slowly stroked her hands down his body, taking illicit enjoyment in the curve of his well-honed shoulders and the erotic dip of his lower back before it flared out into an exquisitely beautiful behind.

"Victor and I have little in common," he said suddenly in the darkness. "So I relate to him through the company. Like boys who play a particular sport just to please their fathers."

She pulled back, seeking his eyes in the muted glow of the moon. "It's your connection. There's nothing wrong with that."

Dimly she was aware he'd squeezed his eyes shut, knew a denial hovered on the tip of his tongue. She held her breath as the seconds stretched interminably. Would he actually voice something that intensely private aloud?

His phone trilled, breaking the moment. With a sigh, he gently disengaged himself from her arms. *Time's up,* the phone continued to mock. *Back to the real world.* As air rushed in to cool her skin, to pebble her nipples, she shivered.

The bed dipped and his feet landed with a soft thump on the carpeted floor and she suddenly realized how she must look—dress bunched at her waist, breasts bare. With a flush she sat up and shoved her hands through her sleeves, barely managing the buttons with stiff, fumbling fingers.

Cal hung up. "I have to go back to Sydney."

"Tonight?" She cringed at the awful, naked neediness

in her voice and ducked her gaze to focus on the last button. Only when it was done did she finally glance up.

They stared at each other, teetering on that finely balanced tightrope as the seconds ticked by. And with those awkward seconds came the inevitable regret and doubt.

Why didn't he say something?

"Okay, you have to go. I understand," she managed as calmly as she could. Yet the clouds of worry that had been temporarily blown away by their lovemaking began to gather in ominous shadows once again.

"Ava, I'm—" He paused, sighed, then started again. "Look, what we—"

"Don't. Don't say anything." Spying her knickers on the floor she quickly snatched them up, cheeks burning. *So help me, if you apologise…* "We had sex. It's no big deal." She forced her voice to sound casual, but her fluttery insides told the real truth.

"Rubbish."

She nearly crumbled then, but pride forced her to remain calm. "It has to be. Look, Cal, let me make this easy. What we did doesn't have to mean anything. We were just two people enjoying sex."

Frustration tinged the edges of his expression, his dark eyes rife with something she couldn't quite fathom. Still he remained silent, just studied her in a way that felt too intense, too intimate, too…*everything* after what they'd just done.

"You have to go," she reminded him.

In uncomfortable expectancy she padded her way over to the en suite. Would he stop her? To her relief, he let her go.

As Ava stepped into the shower and the jets of hot water streamed across her skin, a thousand conflicting thoughts battled for attention in her brain. What on earth had she done? One night of forbidden passion was forgivable, even understandable given the pressures in her life, but twice? And with a man she knew better than to get emotionally entangled with.

She couldn't change him anymore than she could stop herself from wanting him. Their lovemaking and Cal's phone call proved that. And it wasn't her place, her right to try and change him. Women who believed they could were just kidding themselves. Love meant accepting the other person's faults as well as their qualities, not being unhappy with—

The bottle of shampoo dropped from her stiff fingers as realization hit her like a wrecking ball—solid, inevitable and twice as devastating.

No. Nooooo…

She loved him. How the hell had that happened?

Amazingly, Ava's burden became heavier, not lighter, under the weight of distance. His absence forced her to rethink everything.

Doubt and uncertainty rolled around in her head for days, only easing off when Cal's interior design team arrived to discuss Jindalee's makeover.

All too soon it was Thursday night and the luxurious car service was depositing her at Cal's apartment. Standing on the footpath staring up at the shiny apartment complex, she finally allowed the emotion to surge up. And surge up it did, nearly choking her in the process.

She gritted her teeth, clenching her fists inside her coat pockets. She'd had two e-mails since Monday, the first from Jenny, Cal's assistant, seeking confirmation that his design team had arrived. The second was sent at some ungodly hour, him asking how the baby was and confirming her return. No phone call so she could wallow in the delicious warmth of his voice, no personal queries about her health, her feelings.

Work had once again taken him away.

With a groan she screwed her eyes shut, blocking out the apartment lights that now seemed to taunt her.

She wouldn't go to pieces. She had to think of the baby. Her and Cal's baby. A baby he wanted, a baby she already loved. If she couldn't have Cal's love then at least they'd be bonded by this tiny life they'd made together.

But would that be enough?

"Ms. Reilly?"

She glanced at the chauffeur, who was holding the doors open for her. A frozen breeze rushed down the street, sending a shiver over her skin, propelling her forward.

It was time to focus on what she was here for. Jindalee. Her baby's future. If Cal wanted a perfect wife, if that meant dressing up and playacting, so be it. If it also meant ignoring the pleasures they'd shared and squashing those more frequently disturbing urges to touch, to taste…?

She couldn't answer that, not until she was faced with it again. And she sure as hell would not lower herself to scheduling in sex like it was some kind of business appointment.

She absently thanked the driver and pressed the elevator's top-floor button.

When the doors swished open, the apartment's only light came from the aquarium's muted glow.

"Cal?"

The silence was complete. Perversely disappointed, she dropped her bag beside the couch, then swept off her coat.

From inside her handbag, her mobile phone beeped. It was Cal's office.

"Ms. Reilly? It's Jenny."

"Yes?" Ava sat gratefully on the couch arm and unzipped her suede boots.

"Mr. Prescott will be late and told me to tell you not to wait up."

"I see."

"Also, your engagement party is scheduled for the third of July."

"Okay."

Jenny paused as if waiting for something more, then said gently, "Have a good night, Ms. Reilly."

"Wait! Jenny?"

"Yes, Ms. Reilly?"

Ava hesitated, but the desire to know overrode everything else. "Is everything okay? I know One-Click is currently virus-testing and I heard there's a new one doing the rounds…" She bit her lip at the leading question, hoping Jenny would fill in the blanks.

She did. "Yes, we managed to contain it but Mr. Prescott's working 'round the clock to find a cure."

The answer should have allayed her doubts, but when Ava hung up, she knew they hadn't even made a dent. Cal wasn't just avoiding her, he was at work and she was alone and waiting—an eerie portent of things to come.

Automatically she went through the motions of making hot chocolate, the familiar task soothing her troubled mind. She had no right to be angry, but it still didn't stop the aching throb in her heart. What they'd shared at Jindalee was just sex, two people mutually attracted doing what came naturally. A spur-of-the-moment thing. A one-off.

It didn't change the fact that work came first with Cal and he was only marrying her for their child. She needed to get that through her head if she was to get through the other side of this marriage with her heart intact.

She'd survive if she had to. And it was really too soon to determine if this was a permanent thing. If it was…

Her child would not have an absentee father. No way. She'd rather suffer the unimaginable but momentary pain of divorce instead of putting her child through years of heartbreaking disappointment.

Nine

Two weeks later, on the eve of his engagement party, Cal stared out the window of VP Tech at the storm obscuring his view. The Harbour Bridge was barely visible past the slashing sheets of rain pounding down, the Opera House only a well-studied memory beneath the iron-grey sky.

He jerked his gaze from the window to take in the expansive hush of his air-conditioned office.

There was no sudden screech of rosellas, no gentle ping of a kitchen timer. He breathed in deep. Coffee brewed an hour ago left its lingering mark, but besides that, nothing. No baking biscuits, no roast. Compared to Jindalee, everything was filed, sorted and in its place.

Ava had been avoiding him—and not just physically. His inadequate "We have to talk" early one morning was met with a curious look and a shake of her head.

"We've got nothing to say," she'd coolly returned before rushing out the door for yet another scheduled interview.

To his surprise, she'd morphed into a media-savvy ingenue, answering all questions with grace and aplomb. Even when people began to speculate about how they'd first met and her future role in the Prescott family, her facade didn't waver; she'd deftly fielded further enquiries with the skill of a pro. It was like living with an elegant shell of grooming and poise.

He ran a hand over his jaw with a sigh. If he'd hated the parties before, he loathed them now. Ava's smile was too bright, the look behind her eyes too controlled. She was turning into everything he'd assumed she was and he hated it.

Last week she'd hired a wedding planner.

He shoved the computer mouse across his desk with a curse. The joy he took in his work, normally a source of deep fulfilment, had waned. Victor had demanded more of his time and focus while he made another international trip and as a result, Cal's working hours had encroached into his Sundays. He'd come to resent the intrusion even if Ava hadn't voiced one objection at his absence. Her silence on that topic had spoken volumes.

In comparison, Jindalee had been coming along in leaps and bounds. He slumped back in his chair, massaging his bunched neck muscles with one hand. To his surprise he'd become emotionally invested in Jindalee's progress. It was something about commanding a small team, watching them interact and bounce ideas around that gave him a deep and profound sense of satisfaction. Flying west had become filled with joy, not obligation, even if it was purely selfish on his part. Because at Jindalee he got the real Ava, the woman with the infectious excitement, the woman who moved him. She made him feel needed despite her outward show of independence. And despite it all, he *wanted* her to need him.

Suddenly exhausted, he closed his eyes, ignoring the phone as it buzzed insistently on the desk.

Ava was right. It was something about the stunning splendour of the land, the utmost peace and tranquillity that called to him. VP Tech had consumed his every waking moment yet the absence of it was like a calm, welcome lull.

The phone continued to scream and with a soft curse he yanked it up and took the call. But less than half an hour later, his mind wandered again.

Ever since their one night at Jindalee there'd been nothing to indicate Ava would welcome him back in her bed. During the week he'd been up to his eyeballs in VP Tech while Ava had returned to Jindalee. When they were together, they weren't alone. And in Sydney he'd come home late too many times to a darkened apartment and a closed bedroom door, only to shower, change, then go right back to work.

It doesn't have to mean anything more than two people enjoying sex.

Work now forgotten, he steepled his fingers and stared out the window as the rain lashed down. More than once he'd caught her watching him as they silently passed each other in the barely light morning, the longing rawness in her eyes barely visible just before she'd glanced away. She wanted him, too.

And dammit, he was tired of waiting for her to admit that.

"We're due in the boardroom in ten minutes."

Startled, Cal turned to find Victor in the doorway, a file tucked under one arm. Annoyance rushed in, flooding every part of his brain. *I'd give a thousand bucks to be anywhere but here.* Jindalee. With Ava. A strange tightness took possession—panic, frustration and regret all mingled in.

He rose, reluctance in every muscle, every limb. "I'll be right there."

"A pleasure to see you, Mr. Prescott, Ms. Reilly. Most of your guests are already here."

The doorman's warm smile never wavered as he swept open the large doors of the Observatory Hotel's private function room. They were soon engulfed by a party in full swing. From the corner of her eye Ava noticed the subtle glances, the way the other guests pretended not to stare as Cal led her through the impeccably decorated interior.

He made introductions with skilled aplomb, introduced her to a dozen people she'd have no hope of remembering after tonight. Still she kept a smile plastered on, tried to respond with genuine happiness at the multitude of congratulations. This unabashed luxury was so far removed from the simplistic glory of Jindalee; she'd love the opportunity to just absorb the ambiance of this heritage-listed building without the intrusion of the gathered throng, to let the smells and sounds of past history rush over her. But with Cal's hand at her back, searing a brand through her elegant sky-blue halter dress, she could do nothing but keep moving forward.

For weeks she'd perfected the charade until she'd finally managed to ignore those minor earthquakes through her body. It happened when there was skin-on-skin, when Cal casually touched her arm, took her hand, or, on occasion, leaned in to place a searing kiss on her cheek. To onlookers, all very loving and intimate but to her pure temptation buzzed through her blood like the gallons of Bollinger champagne they'd been constantly toasted with. Champagne that was off-limits, she chafed. Cal had had the foresight to fill her glass with sparkling cider and thankfully no one ever seemed to notice.

The night wore on, through Victor's formal welcoming of Ava into the family, Cal's response and a few impromptu speeches from the floor. Then the lights dimmed and someone turned up the music—sexy, energetic, heavy-on-the-bass dance music that throbbed in her temples—and people started migrating to the dance floor.

She was alone for the first time that night, standing with a half-drunk glass of cider, watching Cal as he casually chatted with an eagerly made-up brunette in a tight black dress that looked as though it'd pop if she took a deep breath.

"Not dancing?" Victor appeared at her elbow.

Ava shook her head. "I'm getting a headache, actually."

"That's not good," Victor agreed solicitously.

Ava wasn't fooled by his demeanour. His eyes were way too calculating. Cal had exactly the same look, had perfected that unnerving stare just a little too well. Her head began to throb in earnest.

"Do you need an aspirin?" Victor asked, waving to a hovering waiter.

"No, thank you. I'll just tough it out a little longer."

Victor followed her eyes to where Cal stood, still talking. "Cal hates these things, but for you, he suffers them."

Ava felt her polite smile slide into uncertainty. "Excuse me?"

Victor turned his full attention to her. "He's been courting the press since you announced your engagement, made sure you're both on the top of the invite list to a dozen parties he normally ignores. And he's devoted precious working hours to your bankrupt business. Cal's unfocused and I believe it's because of you." He flicked a glance to her stomach. "And that baby."

Blood pounded through her veins, flushing her skin deep and hot. "How…?"

"Cal told me." Victor turned to give her his full attention, blocking her view of Cal. "And given the kind of man he is, I'm not surprised he offered marriage. But you must also be aware of his commitments, his responsibilities. Tell me, do you know how much he earns?"

She shook her head. "I've never thought about it."

"Over six thousand dollars a minute. Now think about how long he's spent on your business. Time *not* spent at VP. Look at him." Victor stepped back and she drank in the sight of Cal, formally dressed in a black Gucci dress suit and a golden tie, looking way too irresistible. "VP Tech is Cal's life. One day it will be his and he'll need his wife to support him." He raised his bushy eyebrows, eyes deadly serious. "A wife who won't make unreasonable demands, one who understands the time and commitment involved in running a billion-dollar company."

"Like Isabelle."

Victor's face softened for one second before the mask was back. "Exactly."

It was Gum Tree Falls all over again. She just couldn't measure up, could she? He made her sound so…inadequate. She rubbed her temple in earnest now. "I didn't… It wasn't…"

"You look pale, Ava. Are you okay?" Cal was suddenly there, his hand on her back before angrily turning to Victor. "What did you say to her?"

The menace below that rough growl was palpably real

and Ava swiftly put a hand on Cal's arm. His muscles tightened into granite hardness beneath her fingers.

"Nothing, Cal. Just a small headache."

When he snapped his gaze from Victor to her, she caught the remnants of that simmering anger bubbling away in those dark depths before it cleared.

"Do you want to leave?"

Around them, the party was in full swing and the warm air and loud music began to pound inside her head.

I want you.

She nodded, unable to meet his eyes just in case he could somehow read her desperation.

They were out of there and into the limousine in record time, but even with the heat turned on Ava still felt the chilly edges of Victor's conversation all the way to her toes.

"What did Victor say to you?"

"Nothing."

He studied her in loaded silence, a silence that pulled at her resolve, twisting and turning until she had to say something.

"I want to thank you for Jindalee—it's more than I could've ever hoped for. But you have other commitments and it was never my intention to drag you away from them."

The muscles in his face tightened. "So he's been giving you the 'time is money' speech."

"I'm sorry."

He stared out the window as they made their way

down Castlereagh Street. "For what? Victor's been a demanding workaholic as long as I've known him."

"So why do you…"

"Stay?" She noticed the way his jaw clenched. "Sometimes I wonder."

She paused. "Look, it might be none of my business…but something's not right between you two."

He swung his gaze back to her, his expression unreadable in the muted interior. "And you're the expert in family harmony?"

She flinched as the tiny barb hit its mark. "I know when something needs to be talked over, not just ignored."

"Trust me, Victor's not talking. He's more concerned with jetting off to Europe."

They arrived at Cal's building then, cutting off Ava's reply.

She suffered the elevator ride under a cloud of thick tension, wishing for the courage to say a million things, but the mere act of breaking this awkward moment made her sweat. So the questions sat on her tongue, unspoken.

Finally inside the apartment, she watched Cal shrug off his jacket with sleek efficiency before striding into the kitchen. He removed a flat whiskey glass from the dishwasher, muttering something under his breath.

"What?" Ava asked.

"I said, sometimes I wonder why my mother puts up with him. She certainly doesn't come first in his life."

Ava smiled, recalling the night she'd first met the

Prescotts. "You don't know that. They really love each other."

"Yeah. She loved my father, too, but he refused to marry her. When he left, it destroyed her."

The unspoken subtext roared between them but Cal was beyond caring. Love hadn't destroyed him. Instead, he'd used Melissa's betrayal to drive his ambition to greater heights. And now he had everything a man could want—wealth, power, security.

Their child.

"Did your father ever contact you?"

Cal glanced away. "No. Victor went looking for him after he and Mum married." With a shrug that looked a little too casual, he added, "The guy died in a bar fight years ago."

Ava blinked. An outsider would've detected nothing amiss with his calm answer. But she saw the tight muscle in his jaw, the emotion in his eyes so expertly covered. The knife-edge control in his deep voice. And just like that, whatever fear she'd been harbouring disappeared.

"Your father—your biological father—had flaws."

His laugh was so bitter, she could taste it. "You call running out on a girlfriend and your six-year-old son just 'a flaw'?"

"I'm not defending him—"

"Then what the hell are you doing?" His eyes were furious, twin daggers of frustration and anger.

"I'm saying everyone is human. Everyone makes mistakes."

"So why can't you forgive yourself for your sister's death?"

The well-aimed jab hit its mark and she drew in a sharp breath. "That's different."

"No, it's not. You were young, you made a mistake."

"And I paid for it with Grace's life!"

She yelled the last word, startling them both. But when the echo died, the air held a sudden expectancy.

"Don't you think," he said softly, "that Gum Tree Falls has blamed you enough without you joining the club, too?"

He had this uncanny ability to cut right to the heart of her.

She closed her eyes, knowing he'd only been the voice to her own black thoughts. He'd acknowledged her deepest, darkest doubt, one she'd hidden from everyone, including herself.

Lord, those memories still possessed the power to chew her up inside.

"And if it wasn't for your father leaving, your mother wouldn't have met Victor. And you wouldn't have created something groundbreaking, something amazing. VP Tech has taken technology to every school in Australia, even the remote country towns."

His mouth twisted into a bitter smile. "So it's all fate?"

"Just like Melissa was."

He snapped his head up then cursed as his glass smashed in the sink. Gingerly he plucked out the pieces then tossed them in the trash.

"Right. So she's not to blame for faking a pregnancy just so you'd marry her?"

Clarity swept in on the tail end of that revelation. "Is that why…?"

"Why what?"

Her chin went up. "Why you don't trust me?"

Cal's body was tense and wound up tight with fury—at Victor, at this ever-present arousal, at these unsettled feelings of conflict. But her soft question washed over him, dousing his anger and yanking him up short.

She stared at the floor, the perfect-fiancée facade she'd perfected these last few weeks gone. In its place was an expression so raw that he knew she was barely holding together. She blinked, and to Cal's horror he wondered if she was about to cry. Had *he* done that? The thought shamed him.

"No!"

His rough denial snapped her eyes up to him, where she remained still, almost as if holding her breath.

His insides were all jammed up, tense and tight. He didn't want to be like Victor, unable to express his feelings and holding on to this bitter grudge he'd perfected against his stepbrother. He didn't want to be like Ava's father, forcing the ones he loved from his life.

He glanced at Ava's belly, to the draping fabric that hid the gentle roundness from view. And there it was again, a rush of incredulity rolling over him, leaving him vulnerable and raw.

"Melissa loved the attention and the money. She

didn't…" *Love me.* He bit off the words and picked out another bit of broken glass from the sink. He couldn't say that, couldn't leave himself open that way. "She lied to get into my family. I don't make the same mistake twice."

"Cal—" Ava paused, weighing up the wisdom of her next words. His ex had done more than lie: She'd taken Cal for a fool, played on his emotions. That was unforgivable. And it cut deeply that he thought she was like that. "I never intended to blackmail you, no matter what you think."

Despite her racing heart, Ava held his probing gaze steadily. *I need you to believe me.*

"I believe you, Ava."

With a whoosh of breath, she released the pressure gathered in her shoulders, closing her eyes in silent prayer. But in the next instant, they sprang open as she felt Cal's fingers brush her cheek.

Cal had leaned forward and was tucking a stray curl behind her ear. Her heart sped up again, this time with insistent, hot need.

"Cal…"

His hand stilled and when his eyes flew to hers, she caught the want, the desire, before the shutters came down.

At that moment, that exact second, her heart soared. She could have done a dozen things—pull away, stop to analyse what she was doing, what it all meant—but instead she grabbed the opportunity with both hands.

Ava leaned forward and kissed him.

It was a closed-mouth kiss, experimental and tentative. It reeked of caution and fear of rejection but when she pulled back, his hard face reflected none of her fears. His dark eyes only reflected danger, as if she'd pushed her luck too far. It sent a forbidden thrill coursing through her limbs, tingling, exciting.

Fear and desire mingled together. Funny how both emotions could bring her to a standstill. She waited for his next move with breathless anticipation.

As she stood there, looking uncertain, a little scared and so completely out of her depth, Cal's heart flipped. Man, she could destroy him with nothing more than a look from those bright blue eyes.

A rocket surge of lust sped through his blood. It had been too long. He'd practically counted the days, the hours since she'd last been beneath him, since he'd been buried inside her welcoming warmth.

He held out his hand. "Come with me."

The simplicity of his command tripped off his tongue like the most skilful of seduction lines and Ava felt herself go under. The intensity, the sheer decadence in the depths of his chocolate-brown eyes tugged at her restraint as if daring her to refuse, to deny the instantaneous pull they both instinctively felt. And in that instant, everything around them faded into obscurity.

Her fate was sealed.

Cal couldn't remember undressing but must have because he was staring down at Ava reclining on his bed, unashamedly naked with her hands behind her head.

Her lush breasts thrust forward, begging for his touch, the look in her come-hither eyes roaring blood through his veins to his groin.

He paused, imprinting the perfect erotic snapshot in his brain.

"Cal…" Her voice was breathy, proof of her arousal, and when her mouth curved into a languorous smile he didn't have a hope in hell of keeping his distance.

His breath came out on a groan as he settled over her, into her, touching and tasting the creamy flesh. She was flawless, from the curve of her cheek to the shapely legs. Dynamite packed into five-foot-three, curve upon curve of lush woman. And it was all his.

He swept a palm over her stomach, revelling in the gentle roundness before dipping his head to place a kiss over her belly button.

Ava was helpless to resist the tremble that started between her legs, a tremble that took over more than just her flesh—it engulfed her heart in a flood of emotion. *Cal, I love you.* She squeezed her eyes shut as she felt Cal's hands and mouth gently caress her belly, his hot breath scorching, branding her.

When his lips crept lower, she jerked, her breath hissing out in a shocked rush. Against her belly, she felt his mouth curve into a smile.

"Open for me." It was more demand than request yet she did as he bade anyway.

The instant Cal's mouth touched the most private part of her, she sighed, a gentle, anticipatory whisper that ratcheted up his heart and sent blood racing at a hundred miles an hour.

In slow, lazy licks he loved her with his tongue and lips, every single sense drenched in her scent, her taste. He wanted to give more, much more, but when her hips began to rock gently, a maddening yet completely perfect motion, the desperate urge to be inside her forced him up.

Her whimper of protest ended on a satisfied sigh as he quickly positioned himself and drove into her hot welcoming flesh.

And as he loved her deeply, thoroughly, he realized that he'd finally come home.

Ten

"Congratulations. You did it," Victor said gruffly. They stood in the small anteroom off the entryway of St Mary's Cathedral awaiting the arrival of the bride. Inside the church a flurry of guests seated themselves among the pews, murmuring quietly. Doctors, lawyers, property developers—the movers and shakers of Sydney society, Cal noticed. The invites included anyone who'd had dealings with Victor and VP Tech, even those Cal barely knew. In comparison, Ava's guests barely took up two rows.

Outside, the street had been cordoned off to preempt the inevitable traffic jam, but it hadn't stopped the crowd steadily growing all day, forcing the local police to serve as crowd control.

Cal tweaked his perfectly knotted cravat with unfamiliar nervousness. By unspoken mutual agreement Sydney was designated business-only—he had VP Tech, she the wedding, interviews, photo spreads. They'd come together for public engagements and frantic, almost desperate lovemaking in the thin hours of dawn before real life intruded once again.

On the flipside, Jindalee was his guilty pleasure. When he stood on the porch surveying the construction chaos against the stunning post-sunset backdrop, his satisfied smile was dimmed only by Ava's echoing one. They made sweet, leisurely love in her comfortable four-poster and afterward, in the dark, he'd stroke her belly and talk to his unborn child, floored and humbled by how simple life could be. Ava didn't talk about the past or bring up the future and Cal let it go, instead revelling in every stolen moment together.

Today, Ava would be his wife. It didn't matter how the day had come to be, just that it was. That's all that mattered. Not this painfully slow ceremony, not the scores of people he didn't know or care about. And from this day on, he'd—

"Did you hear me?" Victor said now.

"I heard you."

For weeks, Cal had kept a tight lid on his simmering thoughts but now they threatened to boil over.

Not now, not today.

He abruptly turned and caught sight of his mother through the half-open door. Beautiful and elegant in a powder-blue suit and a small-brimmed hat, she stood at the entrance and greeted latecomers with a wide smile.

He grinned, but that fell when Victor pointedly closed the door.

"You've been distracted, unfocussed." Victor continued with a puckered brow. "If you're having second thoughts…"

Cal turned back to the long baroque mirror and straightened his perfectly straight sleeves. "A bit late for that now, isn't it?"

Victor sighed. "Look, that was—"

"I don't care anymore."

"Clearly not."

Cal's eyes snapped to Victor's reflection through the mirror. Sarcasm, mixed with an odd kind of guilt, creased the older man's face.

"We need to talk."

Cal shrugged. "About?"

"The future of the company."

He snorted. "I'm getting married, Ava is having my child. Aren't I doing enough?"

"I have a brain tumour."

The world slammed to a halt. *Victor was sick?* Cal gaped. "What?"

Victor's lip tilt was anything but humorous. "A brain tumour—a slow one, which apparently is the best type to have. I've been seeing a Swiss specialist who's been monitoring it and now he's recommending surgery. It's a tricky operation with obvious risks, but he's confident. I go under the knife next week."

The apprehension eased off a bare inch. "Does Mum know?"

Victor's slight nod barely classed as acknowledgement. "She wanted to tell you weeks ago, but—"

"Damn right I needed to know! Jesus!" Anger bubbled up inside, churning futilely in the pit of his stomach. "So what will you do about…" He trailed off, blood rushing from his face as realization dawned. "So that's where you've been jetting off to. And *that's* why you demanded I get married! Sonofa—"

"You're having a baby and getting VP Tech. Tell me where you lose in this."

Cal clenched his teeth. Never before had he felt the desperate urge to deck another man, sick or not. "You didn't have to lie."

Irritation creased Victor's face. "I didn't lie—I just didn't elaborate. I know you, Cal. You needed an incentive. I wanted you committed—"

"Bullshit. You knew the company was my life, my number-one priority."

"'Was'?" Victor frowned.

"You know what I mean. And don't change the subject."

Victor crossed his arms stiffly. "I wanted you settled. The company just provided leverage."

Cal took a deep breath, forcing the fury back behind the gates. "So you have pangs of mortality and suddenly decide I needed to get married?"

Victor flushed, his eyes skittering away. "A man thinks of lots of things when he's faced with death."

They both paused, two proud men unwilling to shine a light on the dark corners of their emotions, until the panic and worry began to ebb from Cal's tense muscles.

"Did you have any intention of giving the company to Zac?" he said, less harshly.

"I knew you wouldn't fail."

Once, months ago, that simple statement would have been a welcome shot in the arm. But instead of pride, Cal only felt a low, simmering irritation.

Victor continued. "Zac's been ignoring my calls since he walked out. Which you would've known if *you'd* actually called him."

Cal sucked in a breath. Victor Prescott pulled no punches, that was for sure. "So he's not coming to the wedding."

"He declined the invite. That boy is so bloody stubborn."

"Like his father."

Victor glared at him. "Or his stepbrother. I've come to terms with Zac never speaking to me again. But you two should kiss and make up before I die."

Cal scowled. "Don't be so morbid. You're not going to die."

"I'm not planning on it any time soon. And your mother just wants to see you happy—"

"Do *not* tell me she knew about your little scheme."

Victor had the good grace to look uncomfortable. "Not at first."

"Brilliant. That's just brilliant." He raked a hand through his newly trimmed hair, mind whirling.

Someone knocked softly on the door but they both ignored it.

Victor straightened his cuffs and cleared his throat. "So. Now that that's out, I'll need your signature next week to finalise the papers."

Cal stared at him for the longest time, until Victor's brows plummeted. "What?"

"We'll be on our honeymoon."

"Oh, right. Seven days."

"Ten."

"We've got that product development meeting with the Department of Education next month." Victor glanced back to the door as the knock came again.

And this from a man about to undergo major surgery in a week? "Sorry. Can't do it."

"Why not? After today the company's yours, something you've always wanted. It will be your number-one priority and I'll need to get you up to speed with things before I leave. The workload will be crazy, of course, but that's nothing new. Your new bride will understand."

Cal strode to the door, his insides shaken from upheaval. His whole life he'd met his responsibilities, had given two hundred percent to gain Victor's approval. *Never walk away.* That vow had shaped every choice, every decision he'd made. And because of it, he'd cut his stepbrother from his life, a decision he'd never fully forgiven himself for, a decision he'd planned to make right today.

Yet Zac hadn't showed.

Cal had won the prize but at what cost? He'd been lied to, manipulated, and he'd responded by doing the same to Ava. Yes, Victor had had his reasons but it didn't mean it was right.

He'd become so damn focused on work that life was passing him by. He'd become Victor and he hated it.

That realization brought sudden clarity into stark focus. With a firm slant to his jaw he reached for the door handle and twisted.

"You blackmailed me into a marriage I didn't want. But you know what? I don't care right now." He yanked open the door, the hinges screaming in protest. "I'm getting married today—"

Victor tensed. "Cal."

"—and you can take your company and shove—"

"Cal?"

The tremulous question behind him broke through his subconscious, jerked his head towards the soft voice.

Ava stood with her hand raised mid-knock. The strapless, flowing white dress, her hair bunched up under a tiara like some fairy princess, her stunningly beautiful face—it all registered somewhere in his brain, on another level. But it was her expression that cut him to the bone, deep pools of blue set in a pale, haunted expression. Those eyes wounded him more deeply than a thousand betrayals.

She took a step backward, shaking her head. "Is it true? Did you…" Her panicking gaze drifted over to Victor. "Did he…?"

"Now, let's just calm down—" Victor began, until Cal stepped across her eyeline, cutting the older man from view.

"It's not what you think."

Her expression tightened. "But is it true?"

His nod was brief but nothing less than shattering. Ava's face crumpled for one second but in the next, she straightened, a flash of something hard and angry in her eyes as she pulled her shoulders back. Alarmed, he reached for her but she put up a warning hand.

"Don't. I thought this baby was important to you, that *I* was important. But obviously, gaining control of your precious company takes top priority."

"Now wait just a minute—" Victor interrupted but to Cal's amazement, her ferocious glare had him snapping his mouth shut.

She had guts, his Ava. There weren't many people who'd stare down the powerful Victor Prescott.

With a look of pure disgust, she backed away, the white satin skirt swirling around her legs in a flurry. And with that one small movement, she dragged the ground out from under him, crumpling hope beneath his feet. In desperation he scrambled for something to say, anything that would stop her from walking out.

"You'll lose Jindalee."

Instead of binding her to him, it drove her away. The

look she gave, pain mingled with pity, ground the rest of his words to hot dust in his mouth as she kept on backing away.

"Do you think that's all I care about—business? Then you don't know me at all."

Cal jerked forward but she was out the huge chapel doors, hurrying past Isabelle, standing open-mouthed in the vestibule.

Cal sprinted after her. It wasn't over. He could fix this, he could turn that utter horror in Ava's eyes back into the slow blooming love he suspected was lurking below the surface. He—

He came to a halt on the pathway. She'd paused at the white Bentley that had delivered her to the church, a hand on the door. With his blood pounding hard and fast, he sighed, a man spared a reprieve. "Ava. Please, let me explain about—"

"Cal…" The pain in her voice pierced his resolve, sending shards of alarm through his brain. Then she slowly turned and the pale fear etched on her face forced his heart into his throat. She clutched her stomach, her eyes huge. "The baby," she gasped. "Cal, the baby!"

He only just managed to catch her as she pitched forward in a dead faint.

"You look like death warmed over."

Isabelle's gentle voice broke through the swirling blackness of Cal's thoughts and he glanced up. Beside him, on the bed, Ava had been asleep for twelve hours.

Twelve hours in which he'd run the gamut of emotions: despair, regret, self-loathing. Twelve hours in which he'd prayed to every deity he could name, and then some he couldn't. *Let her live. Let our baby live.*

He wasn't surprised he looked like crap.

"The doctor says both she and the baby will be fine," Isabelle said now.

With a curt nod, he dragged a hand over his stubbled chin, words failing him.

When Isabelle gathered him in her arms, he held on tight, letting her rock him gently like he was once again her baby. "They're fine, Cal," she whispered. "They're fine. I'm so happy for you." She pulled back then, dabbing at her eyes with a tissue before composing herself. "Victor's outside. He wasn't sure if you'd want to see him after…well." She waved a hand, letting him fill in the rest.

"You heard."

"Victor told me. He has a convoluted way of showing it, but he loves you. He isn't proud of deceiving you, you know. You're a good man, Cal and I love you very much. But you're also stubborn and unforgiving."

"If you're taking his side—"

"I'm taking no one's side. Believe me, Victor knows how angry I am." Her face softened as she added, "Give him a break—we both had a terrible scare. Can you imagine how he's been since having to face his mortality?"

They both shared the black humour with mutual smiles until Isabelle said, "We talked for weeks—about life, family. Zac. You. We both knew you hadn't been happy in a while. I thought you needed romance and Victor assumed your work wasn't challenging enough."

Wasn't challenging enough? Cal shook his head, harsh laughter bubbling from his mouth.

"Cal?"

Ava's croaky question shot him to his feet. He barely registered his mother's departure, the gentle click of the door behind. Instead his complete attention was on the seemingly tiny figure on the hospital bed.

Her hand went to her stomach, her eyes round with panic. "The baby—"

"He's okay." He took her hand, felt the icy cold beneath his fingers. "You're okay."

"He?"

Cal nodded, too choked up to speak.

"We're having a boy," she said faintly. When her eyes met his, relief smashed down on him like a thousand bricks.

"Jesus, Ava…you…I…"

To his shame, his voice cracked on that last word. And to compound his mortification, he felt the track of tears slide over his cheeks. Flushed, he reached up to dash them away but Ava tightened her grip with a confused frown.

"Cal…did I hear you praying to Buddha?"

He went for a laugh but it came out nervous and unsure. "Yeah."

"And God and Mohammed and—" she screwed her face up in concentration. "—Zeus?"

"I wanted to make sure the message got through."

"Because of me?"

Her eyes were deep and fathomless, eyes he could happily drown in. His heart began to up its tempo, his breath shaky.

"I didn't want to lose you. Or the baby. Ava…" He took a deep breath, snaring her wide gaze in his. "I'm sorry I didn't tell you." She swallowed, the small movement drawing Cal's attention to the smooth column of her throat. "Waiting for the ambulance was the longest ten minutes of my life. And when they couldn't revive you…"

He bowed his head, panic rising up in his throat as the memory engulfed him. The soft pressure of her hand grasping his dragged him back from the edge and he looked up, only to go under again, drowning in those blue eyes.

"I didn't think you needed to know," he began again. "You were marrying me anyway and I…dammit."

Her hand squeezed his. "I understand, Cal. It's okay."

"No, it's not. An omission is still a lie. I…" He hesitated, then said, "I love you, Ava."

She drew in a sharp breath and closed her eyes, almost as if it hurt. In the long, painful seconds that followed, Cal waited, his skin prickling, nerves taut. As he waited, a small tear trickled out and curved over her cheek, before her eyes flew open.

"I love you too, Cal. But…" She paused, took a deep shuddery breath that seemed to come from the depths of her soul. A shard of deep pain crossed her face, wounding him square in the chest. "How can this marriage work? I want to be with you, Cal, because I love you. But your life is VP Tech, it's not with me."

"Sweetheart, I don't want the company. I want you."

Confusion flitted across Ava's face. "But I thought—"

"Yes, I originally wanted to marry you to get the company. But things have changed. I've changed." He massaged her hands gently between his. "I am one-hundred-percent, completely and totally in love with you. And I am one-hundred-percent positive that I don't want VP Tech. I want a life. With you."

Oh. Everything ground to a slow, breath-stopping halt. Ava couldn't move, couldn't speak. In her head, thoughts began to zip crazily around, sending her brain into a whirl.

"Ava?" He smiled, a tentative smile that got her heart racing, her blood pumping. "You're in shock."

"No…yes…I…" Her heart pounded in fury, sending a wonderful tingle through every vein, every limb. This was more, so much more than she ever expected. Ever hoped. Ever wanted.

"Nod if you can hear me," Cal said, his voice dipping low, making her shiver.

She nodded.

"You love me."

Nod.

"Do you want to marry me?"

Nod.

"How does a March wedding at Jindalee sound?"

Nod.

His slow, generous grin melted her bones. "I'm going to kiss you."

She finally managed to breathe. "Wait. Does this mean Zac gets the company?"

"Oh, so now you have a problem with marrying a guy who's unemployed?" he teased, his mouth so close to hers that it made her tremble.

Her lips curved. "You should call him. He walked out on Victor, not you."

"I was planning to. But first you need to shut up so I can kiss you."

"Yes," she managed just before his warm breath feathered into hers and their lips met in a long, languorous kiss.

Epilogue

Two months later

"Well? What did Zac have to say?" Ava said from the bedroom doorway as Cal hung up the phone.

He glanced up, then did a double take. "What on earth have you got on?"

She looked down at her attire, then back up at him with an innocent grin. "Your boxers are nice and roomy. And your T-shirt smells like you. Mmm," she purred, rubbing the sleeve against her cheek with exaggerated delight.

He laughed, tossed the phone onto the couch and crossed the room in long, purposeful strides. As he reached her, the setting sun spread through the window, bathing her in red and gold ribbons. The light bounced off her shoulders and the glints in her freshly washed hair, illuminating her pregnant belly in all its glorious roundness.

He exhaled, slowly and shakily.

"Lord, you're beautiful."

He'd never get tired of seeing her blush. And when he reached out to cup her belly, their eyes met, both acknowledging the joy and power of the life growing inside her.

She tilted up her chin, her lips seeking his, and without reservation he gave himself up to the pure pleasure of their kiss. Her peach-and-vanilla fragrance, now as familiar as the silken skin beneath his fingers, never failed to turn him on. Her willing mouth, her long-limbed beautiful body, now lush and plump with his child... Senses exploded and in record time he was hard, the familiar thump-thump of arousal speeding up his heartbeat, forcing his breath out in ragged gasps.

Ava abruptly pulled back. "What did Zac say?"

Cal groaned, his arms tightening around her. "I'm ready and raring to go and you want to talk about my brother?"

"Hey, mister, you were the one who started kissing me."

"Yeah, but you wanted it." His hand swept down her back and over her butt before coming to rest on her belly. He grinned when he felt her shudder and a tiny groan escaped her kiss-stung lips.

"Cal!"

He sighed with exaggerated grief. "Fine. Zac didn't believe Victor would give up VP Tech or I'd given up the CEO's position." He leaned in and resumed his exploration, placing soft, seductive kisses on her warm nape. Her small pleasure-laden sigh sent a shot of pure male satisfaction through his veins.

"But he's taking the position?"

Cal grunted noncommittally, his attention and mouth now focused solely on where her neck met her earlobe. "That's not clear. He's coming down to Sydney on Friday to sort it all out."

"That's great!" Ava pulled back, breaking contact midkiss. "With Victor now fully in remission it'd do them both good to sort out their differences and—"

"Wife-to-be," he growled, tightening his embrace, "do you want to talk about Zac and Victor or would you rather I take off that ridiculous getup and kiss you all over?"

"Oh."

Ava swallowed. If a girl could melt, she'd be doing it right about now. The hot, possessive look in Cal's eyes made her entire body sing with anticipation, the insistent press from his groin proof positive he wanted her. But more than that, he loved her. Every day he showed her—and not just with gifts she suspected gave him more pleasure to give. It was in the thousand little ways that a commanding, proud man such as Cal Prescott demonstrated love—in the sudden looks, the constant, gentle touching. And in the middle of the night, when they lay spent and satisfied from lovemaking, he'd caress her seven-month bump and talk to their child with such reverent adoration that it brought her to tears every time.

"I have something for you," Cal said with a grin as he turned her around and steered her into the bedroom.

She blinked now, forcing the emotion back. "Cal, really. You don't need to keep buying me things. I've got more than enough clothes and jewellery to last…What's that?"

He'd removed a scrap of black material from his jacket pocket and was dangling it from one finger with a wolfish grin.

"Are those my…?"

"Black satin knickers from our first night together." He hooked two fingers around the delicate waistband and pulled. "Care to try them on?"

Ava rolled her eyes. "They'd hardly fit."

He nodded seriously. "I guess not."

"Cal!"

He laughed as her punch landed on his arm, her balled fist making absolutely no impact upon the knots of honed muscle. With a mischievous gleam in his eye, he wrapped her in his arms and they gently fell to the bed, his body cradling hers.

As their laughter subsided, his face became serious, an expression she'd come to know all too well. Slowly, sensuously, he locked his fingers in hers and pulled them over her head. "I love you, wife-to-be."

She'd never get sick of hearing those words from his

lips. That low, throbbing declaration flooded her senses, filling her with love, clogging her throat with brimming emotion.

"And I love you, husband-to-be." And then with her whole body, her whole heart, she proceeded to show him.

Celebrate Harlequin's 60th anniversary with
Harlequin® Superromance®
and the DIAMOND LEGACY miniseries!

Follow the stories of four cousins as they come to
terms with the complications of love and what it means
to be a family. Discover with them the sixty-year-old
secret that rocks not one but two families in...
A DAUGHTER'S TRUST by Tara Taylor Quinn.

Available in September 2009 from
Harlequin® Superromance®

RICK'S APPOINTMENT with his attorney early Wednesday morning went only moderately better than his meeting with social services the day before. The prognosis wasn't great—but at least his attorney was going to file a motion for DNA testing. Just so Rick could petition to see the child…his sister's baby. The sister he didn't know he had until it was too late.

The rest of what his attorney said had been downhill from there.

Cell phone in hand before he'd even reached his Nitro, Rick punched in the speed dial number he'd programmed the day before.

Maybe foster parent Sue Bookman hadn't received

his message. Or had lost his number. Maybe she didn't want to talk to him. At this point he didn't much care what she wanted.

"Hello?" She answered before the first ring was complete. And sounded breathless.

Young and breathless.

"Ms. Bookman?"

"Yes. This is Rick Kraynick, right?"

"Yes, ma'am."

"I recognized your number on caller ID," she said, her voice uneven, as though she was still engaged in whatever physical activity had her so breathless to begin with. "I'm sorry I didn't get back to you. I've been a little…distracted."

The words came in more disjointed spurts. Was she jogging?

"No problem," he said, when, in fact, he'd spent the better part of the night before watching his phone. And fretting. "Did I get you at a bad time?"

"No worse than usual," she said, adding, "Better than some. So, how can I help?"

God, if only this could be so easy. He'd ask. She'd help. And life could go well. At least for one little person in his family.

It would be a first.

"Mr. Kraynick?"

"Yes. Sorry. I was…are you sure there isn't a better time to call?"

"I'm bouncing a baby, Mr. Kraynick. It's what I do."

"Is it Carrie?" he asked quickly, his pulse racing.

"How do you know Carrie?" She sounded defensive, which wouldn't do him any good.

"I'm her uncle," he explained, "her mother's— Christy's—older brother, and I know you have her."

"I can neither confirm nor deny your allegations, Mr. Kraynick. Please call social services." She rattled off the number.

"Wait!" he said, unable to hide his urgency. "Please," he said more calmly. "Just hear me out."

"How did you find me?"

"A friend of Christy's."

"I'm sorry I can't help you, Mr. Kraynick," she said softly. "This conversation is over."

"I grew up in foster care," he said, as though that gave him some special privilege. Some insider's edge.

"Then you know you shouldn't be calling me at all."

"Yes… But Carrie is my niece," he said. "I need to see her. To know that she's okay."

"You'll have to go through social services to arrange that."

"I'm sure you know it's not as easy as it sounds. I'm a single man with no real ties and I've no intention of petitioning for custody. They aren't real eager to give me the time of day. I never even knew Carrie's mother. For all intents and purposes, our mother didn't raise either one of us. All I have going for me is half a set of genes. My lawyer's on it, but it could be weeks— months—before this is sorted out. Carrie could be adopted by then. Which would be fine, great for her, but then I'd have lost my chance. I don't want to take her. I won't hurt her. I just have to see her."

"I'm sorry, Mr. Kraynick, but…"

* * * * *

Find out if Rick Kraynick will ever have a chance to meet his niece.
Look for A DAUGHTER'S TRUST
by Tara Taylor Quinn,
available in September 2009.

**We'll be spotlighting a different series
every month throughout 2009
to celebrate our 60ᵗʰ anniversary.**

**Look for Harlequin® Superromance®
in September!**

*Celebrate with
The Diamond Legacy
miniseries!*

Follow the stories of four cousins as they come to terms
with the complications of love and what it means to
be a family. Discover with them the sixty-year-old secret
that rocks not one but two families.

A DAUGHTER'S TRUST by *Tara Taylor Quinn*
September

FOR THE LOVE OF FAMILY by *Kathleen O'Brien*
October

LIKE FATHER, LIKE SON by *Karina Bliss*
November

A MOTHER'S SECRET by *Janice Kay Johnson*
December

Available wherever books are sold.

You're invited to join our Tell Harlequin Reader Panel!

By joining our new reader panel you will:

- Receive Harlequin® books—they are FREE and yours to keep with no obligation to purchase anything!
- Participate in fun online surveys
- Exchange opinions and ideas with women just like you
- Have a say in our new book ideas and help us publish the best in women's fiction

In addition, you will have a chance to win great prizes and receive special gifts! See Web site for details. Some conditions apply. Space is limited.

To join, visit us at

www.TellHarlequin.com.

Stay up-to-date on all your romance reading news!

The Harlequin Inside Romance newsletter is a **FREE** quarterly newsletter highlighting our upcoming series releases and promotions!

Go to
eHarlequin.com/InsideRomance
or e-mail us at
InsideRomance@Harlequin.com
to sign up to receive
your **FREE** newsletter today!

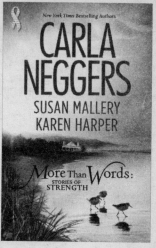

INTRODUCING THE FIFTH ANNUAL
MORE THAN WORDS ANTHOLOGY

Five bestselling authors
Five real-life heroines

A little comfort, caring and compassion go a long way toward making the world a better place. Just ask the dedicated women handpicked from countless worthy nominees across North America to become this year's recipients of Harlequin's More Than Words award. To celebrate their accomplishments, five bestselling authors have honored the winners by writing short stories inspired by these real-life heroines.

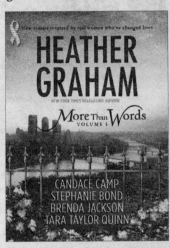

New stories inspired by real women who've changed lives

HEATHER GRAHAM
NEW YORK TIMES BESTSELLING AUTHOR

More Than Words
VOLUME 5

CANDACE CAMP
STEPHANIE BOND
BRENDA JACKSON
TARA TAYLOR QUINN

Visit **www.HarlequinMoreThanWords.com**
to find out more, or to nominate
a real-life heroine in your life.

Proceeds from the sale of this book will be reinvested in Harlequin's charitable initiatives.

Available in April 2009 wherever books are sold.

REQUEST YOUR FREE BOOKS!

2 FREE NOVELS
PLUS 2
FREE GIFTS!

Passionate, Powerful, Provocative!

SDES09R

Silhouette Desire

COMING NEXT MONTH
Available September 8, 2009

#1963 MORE THAN A MILLIONAIRE—Emilie Rose
Man of the Month
The wrong woman is carrying his baby! A medical mix-up wreaks
havoc on his plans, and now he'll do anything to gain custody of
his heir—even if it means seducing the mother-to-be.

**#1964 TEXAN'S WEDDING-NIGHT WAGER—
Charlene Sands**
Texas Cattleman's Club: Maverick County Millionaires
This Texan won't sign the papers. Before he agrees to a divorce, he
wants revenge on his estranged wife. But his plan backfires
when she turns the tables on him....

#1965 CONQUERING KING'S HEART—Maureen Child
Kings of California
Passion reignites when long-ago lovers find themselves in each
other's arms—and at each other's throats. Don't miss this latest
irresistible King hero!

#1966 ONE NIGHT, TWO BABIES—Kathie DeNosky
The Illegitimate Heirs
A steamy one-week affair leaves this heiress alone and pregnant—
with twins! When the billionaire father returns,
will a marriage by contract be enough to claim his family?

#1967 IN THE TYCOON'S DEBT—Emily McKay
The once-scorned CEO will give his former bride what she
wants...as soon as she gives him the wedding night he's long been
denied.

**#1968 THE BILLIONAIRE'S FAKE ENGAGEMENT—
Robyn Grady**
When news breaks of an ex-lover carrying his child, this
billionaire proposes to his mysterious mistress to create a
distraction. Yet will he still want her to wear his ring when she
reveals the secrets of her past?

SDCNMBPA0809